Christopher Martinez

Perfection Is Key

AUTHOR'S NOTE
This book contains foul language.

The following story is based on quite the mental journey I faced during a hard time, and I felt like this is the place to show you what was thought of, said, and done.

Mental Health surely is a serious topic. I'm sure we all know that. And one thing for sure is that we live in a world where young men don't know how to be leaders. They are living in a world that makes them think they need to be handsome, physically fit, and appealing to the finest. A world where showing emotions makes you a weak man.

All kinds of men can shield themselves from emotions because they fear something, or because they were raised in a world where being "manly" for everything is the key. And in this story, it's where being popular and following trends is the key.

There are too many days that I have felt unworthy of life. It's become so common that men are trashed, and no man has anything to say about it. I can't fathom the ugly feeling of self-hate and pity whenever I am asked why I exist.

Us men are strong, smart, and handsome in our own ways. Stand out and be your own self. Be open and cling for strength when you fall to your knees. You have the choice to help yourself with recovery, but always know you don't have to face it all alone.

Christopher Martinez

Copyright © 2021 by Christopher Martinez

All rights reserved. This book or any portion thereof may not be reproduced or used in any manner whatsoever without the express written permission of the publisher except for the use of brief quotations in a book review.

First Printing, 2021

Perfection Is Key

*TO MY YOUNGER SELF,
YOU ARE ENOUGH.*

Christopher Martinez

Perfection Is Key

Chapter One
The New Guy in Town

Usually, a regular story would begin with "once upon a time," but here comes something different. But before this story continues, it may slowly start to sound like another typical, boring old story of the movie, "Mean Girls." But let's just focus on the real part here. It gets real and interesting. Not to mention that there's death involved. Just remember to be perfect.

Zander Robbins was a young man who was headed towards his junior year of high school, but unfortunately, he ended up spending it at a different school. His parents had started a new job in an unknown small city that was out in the middle of nowhere. They called it Rampage. The name itself should give a shiver. This city was very elegant for anyone to even breathe in its soul.

  As for the Robbins, Simon and Melissa were not entirely ordinary parents. In fact, they kept a very dirty secret from their only child, but we'll talk about that later.

  As of right now, I'm going to tell you the story of how Zander's world went from sunshine and rainbows to black skies and thunderstorms.

  You see, Zander wasn't too happy to move, but he was willing to make sure that anywhere he went, he would bring his

Christopher Martinez

strength and his kindness. Not only did leaving his hometown make him upset, but the sad fact that he had to leave his best friend behind was even worse.

Ryan Williams was that handsome boy that just wished to live like any other person. He was some type of hunk to everybody, but he never gave in to things like that. He was someone special. Someone uniquely different. It's kind of the reason why Zander chose him to be his best friend.

"Man, I hate to burst your bubble, but this Rampage is just too good to be true," he said while talking with Zander through the video chat. Zander never wanted to believe a word he said. That is until everything hit him like the heaviest rock.

Rampage High is...well, perfection. And no matter what words you preach, nor the actions you imply, perfection was always the key.

Zander began unpacking his bags as his computer was already set up and opened wide for him to video chat with Ryan. Ryan continued speaking.

"I'm sorry for seeming like a buzzkill, but bro, that school is NOT any regular school. It's full of arrogance. After that one year when my cousin Jack attended classes there, he told me that someone once went into the principal's office and then never came out." Zander rolled his eyes and closed his dresser doors as he sat in front of the screen.

"Look, I think my parents would know if this city was too shallow, and it's not. It's just one of those very fancy places. I mean, it is rich. I hear some of the restaurants here sell Italian food! How awesome is that?!"

Perfection Is Key

"What about the people? Have you met, or seen one person? The moment you get to know someone, I bet everything might just come crumbling down." Zander chuckled as his mother suddenly walked in.

"Hey sweetie! Hi Ryan!"

"Oh, and in comes the Queen," said Ryan through the screen. Zander glared at him while slightly shaking his head.

"I hope you boys aren't plotting any trouble," said Melissa.

"Of course not, mom. We were just talking about school. Which apparently is like the danger zone," said Zander. His mother intensively grasped his shoulders as a huge smile brushed over her face.

"Oh, I am so excited for this new journey! I sure hope you've prepared for it cause it's going to be quite the ride. Anyway, I better let you finish unpacking. Your father and I must do some other things before we finish the paperwork for your classes. Dinner will be later tonight, okay? Bye!" She stepped out as Ryan waved and Zander just smiled.

He then grabbed his head and made a dramatic frown. He began to think about all the homework, thinking it could be more intense when coming from a rich school. Ryan suddenly interrupted his thought process.

"Bro, I'm telling you, trust nobody! Those students are nothing ordinary! They only make the worst of you, so please just stay in closed groups, keep your distance, and focus on your dreams! Alright?"

Christopher Martinez

"Thanks, but what exactly gives you this thought that they would be killer monsters, or something?" Zander responded with a slight chuckle.

"You know me, I don't think about things, I know because it's what Jack has informed me about." Zander chuckled at him as he heard his mother call him from downstairs.

"I'll be fine, alright? They're just people, not God. I'll talk to you later, okay?"

"For sure! But don't say I didn't warn you," he replied with an eyebrow lift. The two said their goodbyes as Zander headed downstairs.

As Zander was about to step on the living room floor, he found a young girl with a cute smile standing with his parents. She wore a tanned top with a skull across it, dark jeans and shoes, and short hair to complete her style. She seemed to be a chill kind of girl.

"Zander, meet our neighbor's daughter, this is Samantha Shaw." Melissa said. Samantha seemed sweet, and she had a kind presence. A beautiful smile to charm Zander's soul, that's for sure. Just at first sight, Zander was already crushing. She stretched out her hand and began to speak.

"Hi. I just thought I'd introduce myself. I know it must be weird moving from a small town to a rich town, but trust me, it can be comforting. It feels great to have new neighbors. The last family that lived were all just a little stingy."

The Robbins became close with Samantha and loved her personality. Although she had given some warnings about a few dangers at the school. As Ryan intended through the video chat,

Perfection Is Key

she seemed to replay his words, but in her own form. This made Zander worry a bit. Luckily though, Zander was informed enough and knew just what to watch out for. Keeping his distance, making good friends, and striving for the best he could do.

It was officially his first day, although he was already halfway through the month of October, he wasn't ready for what the school had in store for him. He was in for one awful treat.

 He walked through the doors. They were like masterpieces. Doors in which you would find at a castle, not at all at a school. The building was clean, shiny, filled with designed floors, objects, and the most stunning students. He was shocked to see all these outfits and accessories that laid on these perfect bodies. Not even the teachers wore anything seductive, or basic.

 The walls were full of gold, and everyone basically wore the word "expensive" across their chests. Zander scanned his surroundings as he found a group of students whispering among each other and laughing while staring at him. There was a guy pulling small trophies from his backpack and placing them into his locker. There were two girls strutting down to a group of jocks as their outfits sparkled and their butts stuck out.

 The material on everyone's clothing and the material that made up their clothes was something you wouldn't find at any normal store. Everything was fancy, elegant, and uncommon. Now no one else was wearing what Zander would call his own looks, garbage. Number one rule here, normal must not be

Christopher Martinez

anywhere near the entrance of the school doors. He turned his head and noticed their school phrase.

"Beauty is your blood. Vain in your veins. And perfection is always key!"

Who on earth would think of such a selfish motto, am I right? The students had started taunting him one by one. Their eyes gave it all away. Their movements and silent judging gave him a haunting chill.

"Dude, what's with the trashy outfit?" said one student.

"Clean it up, you look like one of those basic bitches," said another.

"What are you wearing, year one?" asked another.

"Are you trying to title us as fools?" continued another.

Zander was sensitive, and anyone who really knew him, knew he was super sensitive to almost anything. Even if it was to be used as a joke. He was hurt, but he suddenly knew he was in a deep ditch. He slowly walked toward his locker by following the guides on his paper. Everyone was pointing, and gossiping, and laughing at him. He began to head toward the nearest restroom instead.

He rushed in, and he slammed the door and let out a deep sigh. He walked up to the sink and stared into the mirror. He felt his heart fall as he stared at himself. He could think only the worst about himself.

'What's wrong with me? My face? My hair? Was I just too quiet? God, I sound like a crazy guy. C'mon Zander, pull it together.'

Perfection Is Key

Suddenly, three stall doors opened. Three handsome young men walked out and gave the most cunning look. Zander rushed up to them.

"Do I look okay?! Wait, maybe I should get a different haircut huh?!..." Zander's first impression came off too desperate. "I'm so sorry. Hi, I'm Zander Robbins, the new guy. It's my first day, so I guess I'm just kind of nervous."

Zander was wearing a beanie, a rock-hard shirt, fancy bracelets, dark blue jeans, and a pair of simple vans. Apparently, it wasn't the look. Standing amongst these three guys was almost like standing in front of a feared king.

"Dude, first off, you could take a step back. You sure you're not lost little guy?" said the first guy as he shot Zander a disgusted face. The other two guys followed all in his track.

"What's up with these puny arms? You know, I wouldn't recommend eating too much, but you could at least make it average. It needs more bulk. Yes! I can see it now. You should join the gym downtown. Maybe we could work something out."

"Yeah, well, even that outfit doesn't work. Are you trying to ruin your own image? C'mon man. You want my advice, get rid of the hat, put on some cooler shoes, and maybe even a rocking hot, leather jacket."

Zander was confused for the moment. But he was too busy being mesmerized by everything around him.

They each shoved him towards the side as he then grabbed his backpack and ran out.

Before he could try to reach for his locker, he ran into a very bright, stunning young girl. She wore a sparkly dress while

Christopher Martinez

her hair was rich, dark red. It was long and curly. Her makeup spoke blossom as it gave off a luscious vibe. She smiled and laughed.

"Oh! Sorry about that. Sometimes I'm never paying attention to my surroundings. You must be Zander Robbins. New kid, right?" She asked.

"Y-yeah. How'd you know?" he replied with a heavy breath while trying to position his backpack comfortably upon his shoulder.

"Lucky guess. I'm Alyssa Reed. I'm kind of like the office aid around here. If anyone ever has questions or is needing some guidance about Rampage, I'm the girl." She laughed a bit as she continued. "So, I see you already have the whole school messing with you. Such a classic thing here. Not me. I'm here to help. I know you're new, so how about I give you some tips on how to survive these halls?" Zander felt unsure about it all, but he managed to walk alongside this girl. After all, she was his only friend right now. He nodded his head and the two began walking down the hall.

"Uh, is this school always like this?" asked Zander.

"Always, and forever. Let's start simple, rules."

"Rules. Okay." His heart felt a little lighter. Though, he wasn't even sure if there were rules.

"Yes. Rampage High is quite the place to be. It has lots of perfection, and now that you're here, we own you." Alyssa said with an eyebrow lift and a small smirk. Zander could only feel weirded out.

Perfection Is Key

"That's a bit harsh, don't you think? I mean, it's just a school. I mean, what's up with the Hollywood glitter bomb up in this place?"

"Maybe your eyes see a Hollywood bomb, but here, it's either perfection or get out. The owners of this school can be cruel if they don't get their way. Talk to me when you have that experience."

They continued walking until Alyssa led him down a hall that was covered in the most enticing wallpaper of gold along with statues of the honored students among Rampage.

There were also pictures and awards for the special students, or most loved if you will. Zander's eye had caught sight of the very end, where three huge statues that stood in pride. He read the name "P3" upon the plaque and then read the following names.

Dylan Anderson, James Coleman, and Liam Dixon. He stared closely at the faces and realized who they were.

"Hey, I think I know these guys. I just saw them in the restroom. They're some honored students?" he asked. Alyssa's eyes dropped in disappointment.

"Ooh P3. Not just honored students, the gods of the school. My best advice: avoid them at all costs. Dylan is the leader of that group and he's one of the owners of the school. Well, he and his family. But to sum it all up, Dylan's the worst person to ever walk these halls."

Zander laughed at her words as he sort of rolled his eyes.

"Are you serious? How bad could he be? You know, back in my hometown, we had this kid named 'Nick' who would do

Christopher Martinez

the most dangerous things to other students and teachers. After years of constant gateway, they had finally sent him away to military school!"

"Cute story, but these guys are nothing like Nick. Just stay away from them, please. They're never worth your time." She stared at the statues as her body sort of shivered. She then turned her attention away.

Zander then turned his head to catch a small, framed piece of newspaper. It was a short story about the birth of Rampage. It was framed in rich gold, with one picture of the tiny town, and another with the owners. He creased his eyebrows as he tried to read the small words on the paper.

"Wow. It's almost like being in Paris or something. This city is crazy gorgeous. Is this really what the houses looked like back in 1990?" Zander asked as Alyssa sort of smiled and tilted her head at the sight.

"Yeah. That was when everything was good. It still had its rich appearance, but it was a good, humble kind of rich. If that even makes sense," she said with a chuckle.

"What do you mean? Did something bad happen?"

"On June 18th, 1990, that was the day that Rampage became such a loving town. Its population grew over the years quickly and it was just… home. But there were some accidents and drama that raged through the Shue's household. Principal Shue is the creator of this lovely city, and he was married to a wonderful lady. Well, during the year of 2012, Mr. Shue's wife had gone and cheated on him while getting drunk, but not only that, she was having an affair with two other guys. After a couple of years of having no more contact with Mr. Shue, she eventually divorced him by writing a note that was attached to a small basket. That basket contained a baby. That's when she announced to him that she was running away and was sorry and of course, that she was pregnant. She had also mentioned that she went into great research in order to make sure that she knew who the father was, and it was for sure him."

"Wow, that sounds awful. I've heard horrible stories before, but none like that. I bet Mr. Shue was heartbroken."

"Yeah, but that wasn't it. Mr. Shue was so depressed that he didn't even want to keep the baby and so he gave him up for foster care. He really loved him, but he wasn't ready. Everyone knows that the kid goes to school here, but no one's ever gotten clues or ideas as to who it could be. He just knew that he'd be a terrible father at the time. And ever since then, the school and the city have become an area for many to get away from reality and just be popular and rich. Its name and location became very secretive and since it didn't reach a whole lot of people, Mr. Shue took advantage and made it the way it is. It's a little confusing. A lot of us think that maybe he's secretly working with his son and his son was the person who wanted to make this city his own personal little kingdom. And overall, Mr. Shue uses it to release his anger and to feel better at keeping everybody here. Where no one can leave him."

Zander felt a bit uneasy. He stared around the walls as he seemed to be tense. His heart felt like it could jump out of his chest. He swallowed.

"Wow, looks like normal has died."

Christopher Martinez

Chapter Two
Neighbors Know Best

Rampage High was not the school for Zander. It was a cruel world, that's for sure. But what did this mean now for him? What was the next move for Zander? Did this mean he must buy new clothes and try to at least fit in somehow? He was surrounded by perfection that was too good to be true. It was a shiny, fake world. Not to mention Samantha Shaw. But that's another secret for later. What was strange to Zander is that Samantha dressed normal and looked normal. Like any regular person you would see at his old school. You would find her wearing baggy shirts, ripped jeans, and spiky wristbands to complete her fashion. Her hair was short and straight and sometimes looked messy.

Monroe High was Zander's old school, but now that he had transferred to Rampage, things are turning around, and the creepiest part, Samantha, was never seen at school. This made Zander worry and question how she was still going to school and living in town anyway. Was she homeschooled? Who knows, but things started to become a little better when Sam gave some good advice to Zander.

By the next day, the two ended up at his house as they discussed a few things about the school.

"So, how long have you been living here?" asked Zander.

"About ten years now...my parents are in love with this city, so they say. I don't believe them half the time considering they complain about a lot of things here and there." She stood off to the side with her hands intertwined. He chuckled at her.

Christopher Martinez

"Well, do you go to school here? I mean, obviously, but I'm just asking. I don't want to sound like I'm some sort of stalker, but I noticed you weren't at school yesterday."

"Well, yes, I do go to school here. And I'm sorry I didn't catch you on your first day. I had some classes and assignments to really catch up on. Although, I'm sure I can help you out in the upcoming days. Maybe." Her voice didn't sound too sure.

The fact that this girl had confessed to attending the school made Zander wish she were there on his first day, but he also questioned more about how she had not been picked on like he was. Maybe she got over it all? Zander sure was curious about her life. He suddenly felt the urge to confess to her.

"How do you handle all of this? The perfection?" he asked.

"Perfection? Of what, the skills and potential? I have better ways to succeed at almost anything rather than being perky or being a quarterback. I'm my own uniqueness. Something that you can find exceedingly rare in this world. Plus, my mom inspires me with her confidence."

"Well... that's what I mean. It's more like barbies, preps, jocks, and full-on perfection. As if everything must be at its finest. Shoot, even the nerds don't look terrible!"

"Oh, that stuff is in every school. My mom always told me to never compare myself to others, and to not interfere with douchebags. Every school year has just been okay and regular, I guess." She laughed while taking a seat on the edge of the bed. She folded her hands in her lap.

Zander was not in his comfort zone, that's for sure. All he was thinking about was a way to understand why Rampage was such a cruel place to be in.

Perfection Is Key

What was the deal with being a perfectionist and not loving what you're created to be? His stomach twisted and his mind flooded with some horrible memories. He felt uneasy.

"Are you okay?" she asked worryingly.

"Yeah. I just need to go to the bathroom. I'll be right back." He stood up and headed toward the restroom and dialed up Ryan. His heart pumped like crazy.

"Hey man, how's it going?

"Ryan, it's me, look I've been thinking about what you said, and it's all coming true! I met a few people and the first three were a bit unhappy with me being there. I've heard rules and some creepy stories that are just making me regret ever walking in!" Ryan leaned forward from his chair.

"Wait, what do you mean? Are you injured? I'll go juice a bitch's head!"

"Nah man, at least not yet. Look, I met my neighbor, Samantha, she dresses and looks exactly the way I would, or anyone would at Monroe, yet she goes to Rampage, and everyone at Rampage is a freaking model!" Ryan became confused.

"What? That school is too cruel to hold anyone like that. Is she new, too?"

"Dude, she's been going here for already ten years!" shock grew to Ryan's eyes.

"Okay, that's impossible. She should've been out of there by day one. No student can handle a life of misery and hate. Wait, I got an idea."

Ryan was informed enough and had heard enough. He started hacking into the school and listed all its students. By all class pictures, he could see every headshot. The faces tried their best to look so innocent and pure.

"Don't tell me you're hacking into the school," said Zander.

Christopher Martinez

"Are you really assuming? Bro, this school has hundreds of people throughout the years. I'm not too for sure if I can find this girl, but if I do, I'll let you know."

"C'mon man, you know I don't like when you do that. One of these days you're going to get your ass caught!" Ryan could barely pay any attention to the words coming out of Zander's mouth. His typing was so fast, he could barely hear what was happening on the other line.

"Okay, so what was your neighbor's name again?" he asked while typing on his computer.

"Samantha Shaw," Zander replied.

Ryan started using his scanning eyes and searched for earlier years but could not seem to find her specifically.

"Man, there is no one listed at all on these lists. Rampage has never had a student named Samantha Shaw. I don't think you can trust this girl. She could be a tracker or something. She may just be playing you like all the rest." Zander widened his eyes and started putting all kinds of thoughts into this head. He stared at the mirror and breathed heavily. A sudden bang on the door. A scare to his heart, luckily it was the voice of his own mother.

"Zander, honey, are you doing okay in there?" she asked.

"Uh, yeah...just a bit lightheaded."

"Okay, well Samantha is waiting downstairs," she replied while walking away.

"I know. I'll be out in a moment," he replied with a beating heart.

As Zander's embarrassment grew, he looked away from the mirror and left. He saw his mother down the hall, she wore a long, black dress. He noticed a black pocket wrapped around her leg.

"What's that?" he asked as she quickly covered it with her dress.

Perfection Is Key

"Oh, it's just umm... You know, one of those fancy ways of holding my things other than my purse. Listen, your father and I have some paperwork to do so we'll be out tonight. I expect nothing from this house by nine, we clear?" He raised his hands in surrender as they each smiled.

"Alright then. Love you sweetie," she finished.

"Honey, can we get some of that chicken salad? I mean, we're going to be working late!" hollered Simon from downstairs. Melissa pinched Zander's cheek and left.

Zander headed downstairs to talk with Samantha as she sat in the center of the couch and admired the beauty of the home.

"Wow, I didn't think you guys would have such...material and class. The decorations and lighting are nice. I really am loving the chandelier."

"Nah, it's really nothing. My parents were once rich and now they still gain lots of money, just not enough to design, or dazzle the place really."

The two spoke for the rest of the evening and it became late. Samantha gave a handshake and headed out.

The rest of the night sort of left Zander in boredom and worried at the fact that his parents were still out late. They were to be home by nine, but I guess things seem to have changed the plans. Zander was a hopeful person though, so he went to sleep knowing his parents would return.

It had become the next day for Zander, and he was very unprepared for whatever was in store for him. He walked in and still gained the same reactions from the students. Including the teachers.

It was third period, and Zander had his class with his new friend, Alyssa.

Christopher Martinez

"Looks like you're still in bad shape," she said while smiling and setting down papers.

"Yeah, I guess," he replied.

"I'm telling you; I'd move quickly and get myself together. Before you know it, this school will destroy you the best way possible, it will terrorize your career path, and life. It won't stop until it destroys everything in which you find joyful. Just saying from experience." Her face fell as the pain covered her face.

"I don't need to change how I look! I don't see why we must follow this dump! Something must be done. We really need to just change the way things are done around here."

"Trust me on this. You don't want to start another war with Principal Shue. Or even worse, Dylan." She patted his shoulder and sat straight in her desk as class began. The teacher began talking as she had this perk within her voice.

"Alright class! How's everyone feeling this morning?" she asked.

"Perfect as usual," said one student.

"Same here," said another.

"Oh, how delightful! It's amazing to be a queen, isn't it? Anyways, Clarissa, I see you've earned those dazzling new boots. Told you they give you great power."

"Of course, Mrs. Taylor! I've already kicked a few lame girls to the curb. They're now scraping the bottoms of my feet every two hours." The girl said with a strong smirk.

Zander leaned forward to see the shoes and it just so happened to be true. These boots were covered in diamonds, glam, while the texture was so leather like and had a shine to its appearance. He whispered to Alyssa as they spoke about how charming they looked.

Perfection Is Key

"And Josh! That new cowboy outfit on you just makes me sparkle inside," continued Mrs. Taylor.

The dude was wearing leather pants along with dark shades, and with his so-called cowboy hat. His jaw was the most enticing thing about him. His tanned skin had blended so perfectly with his bling. Zander was so confused to see how everyone treated themselves with such adoring eyes. It was sickening.

The teacher smiled until her eye became stuck to Zander. He stiffened in his own seat as his heart pumped a bit. She lowered her glasses.

"This must be our new student. Zander Robbins. I've been hearing so many awful things about you. They weren't kidding when they said you could use some improvement. Maybe some more bone structure, and some more color. Oh, you would be one of those honored students, but too bad you'll never stoop to anyone else's level." The class began laughing as Zander felt his heart drop. He turned his head towards Alyssa as she shook her head slightly, warning him not to get involved in any form. He turned back and gave a smile.

"Mrs. Taylor, am I right? Don't you think that's a bit too harsh to say to a student? Not only am I a student, but I'm also a person you know."

"Well, I don't really care what you say you are. Nothing here is harsh, what is said is true! You're just going to have to deal with that. Go stand in the front for me."

"The...the front? Of the class?" he said with a shaky voice. He awkwardly walked up to the front and smiled faintly at everyone as they all gossiped and teased him. He became really shy within seconds. Mrs. Taylor gave a malice smile.

"Now tell me, how does it feel being the one looking real foolish to these people. How embarrassing!"

"Excuse me, but I-"

Christopher Martinez

"Oh kid, don't you get it? You're nothing. What you've brought into my classroom is pure garbage! God, I feel terrible for your parents! How do they deal with this?"

"I will have you know that I am perfectly fine the way I am!! Other than showing curves to prove you're a hoe, or muscle to prove you're a selfish man! You think all of this is gold? Trust me...you'll all rot like the rest of us." Zander's blood was now boiling.

"No, what you have is a flat purpose for even existing! Maybe I'll send a card to your family telling them how sorry I am. Now sit down. I've been feeling nauseous too much already."

All the kids were laughing once again, or chuckling, while whispering their mouths away with each other. Alyssa lowered her eyes in sympathy. Zander grew sudden anger, but also felt a little fear. He was now face to face with Mrs. Taylor.

"Yeah? Just sign your name regularly, it's easier to read a bitch's name that way."

"Ooooo," said the students dramatically in unison. Her face dropped as her eyes widened. She shoved him aside and grabbed a slip for detention. Zander grabbed his things and left the room.
Alyssa sighed.

"Oh Zander. What did you do?" she said to herself.

Chapter Three
Home For the Day

A fresh new Friday and so far, the Robbins Family have had no problems in the city, at least two of them haven't. Zander was dealing with negativity in such a way that made him feel so alone. It was only the first Friday of being a so-called "trashy" member of Rampage and Zander was sent to the principal's office. Not the place you want to be when you're the lame guy of a so-called "perfect" world.

"Ugh, you are one of the many reasons why I hate doing this job. But being the head of this place makes it comfier. So, you've called a teacher a name which causes a whole month of after school detention. And if you don't even show up, I will have to go door to door and hunt your ass down. If you want to stay in this school, you had better start following the rules. Otherwise, there's going to be consequences and we all know what some of those can lead to." He gave a dead smile to him while rearranging papers on the corner of his desk.

"Well, I didn't mean to call her anything, I mean I was just angry, and I don't know, I guess I was crowded with so many thoughts at the moment."

Mr. Shue chuckled at him as he leaned back in his seat, which looked nothing like an office chair, but a royal palace chair with the arms chiseled in the form of a lion's face.

"Yeah, I don't really give a shit. If you just follow along the schedule of being in detention, then we're good afterwards. Now go back to class. And for once, pick a better outfit," he screamed while

Christopher Martinez

rubbing his eyes. He leaned back into his seat as Zander could feel his insecurity grow once more. He swung his backpack over his shoulder and headed out.

After school, Zander was so excited for the weekend. It was a deserved break from everything he had already been through. And around four-thirty, Zander's parents had announced that they were going to visit home for some sort of 'special occasion.'

This grew Zander with excitement as he packed up a few belongings and went along on the trip. He was more excited to see Ryan. He planned on staying the night over as his parents went along on their little event.

After a couple of hours, Zander found himself standing at the front door. He knocked and knocked as he waited eagerly.

"Go away! I told you; I'm married," yelled Ryan from the other side. Zander furrowed his brows.

"Ryan! It's me man!"

Just by that voice, Ryan leaped from behind the living room wall. He quickly opened the door as a huge smile brushed over his face.

"Yo! My brother! What are you doing here, man?!"

"My parents are doing something for their business, so I get to spend the weekend here!"

"Nice! Well, c'mon! We've got to catch up on so many things! Alright, so tell me, what's everyone like? Are you doing good with grades and stuff? How's the football team, or the girls? How about the food? Is the toilet paper really in a cube shape instead of a roll?"

"Well, for starters, the city is crazy beautiful! And I mean, that may be the bright side of it all, but you were so right about the school and its people. It's like walking into a virtual world where the entrance suddenly whirls away! It's all about the bling for them."

Perfection Is Key

"I told you! Look, I've been thinking that maybe we can try and find a way to expose this town and show the police what it does to its students and how it abuses everyone's minds. We'd be able to get rid of the whole place and make sure no one ever gets taken hostage there ever again." Zander smiled at the thought. Ryan continued. "But we'll deal with that later, as of now, what do you know about Samantha? Have you found anything else about her?" Zander ran his hand through his hair with a slight smile.

"Oh. I haven't. I've been swamped with all this thinking. I mean, she's sweet, she's pretty, and she knows how to give a helping hand. I just haven't given her much thought lately."

"But it seems she's hiding something about how she's still surviving this tragic career. You know, I've done some research on this school and let me just say, it's been disturbing."

Ryan grabbed his laptop and placed it onto his laps. Opening the internet full of stories. The computer was covered with pages and small tabs telling stories of horrifying deaths, or unsolved cases.

"16-year-old dies at Rampage High from overdose."
"Kacey Plum, former student of Rampage was secretly found hanging from a tree."

Zander's stomach began to twist with aches.

"God, that sounds terrible," he said. He toppled while walking towards Ryan's bed.

"Whoa, bro, you good? Sorry, I didn't mean to scare you like that." Ryan placed his hand on Zander's shoulder as he tried to comfort him. Zander stood back up with a smile.

"I'm fine. I guess this school was just much worse than I thought. How can something be such a deadly place that it kills its own people? It's just sad."

Christopher Martinez

"Forget about it man. They can't do anything to you. You're too strong for them to break," said Ryan.

"It doesn't feel like it sometimes. They've got quite the power over me. I really think we should put a stop to all of this. I don't want people to live in a world that makes them feel wanted but are not wanted..." Ryan made a huge smile and patted his back.

"Already covered."

Meanwhile, Simon and Melissa Robbins were out running their paperwork. Truth be told, they were on a secret mission to stop some bad guys from robbing a bank. Yes, they were spies. They've been in this game for almost twenty years now. Stopping bad guys from robbing, committing murder, sex trafficking, and more. Zander didn't know due to him being in great danger if he did. The two love birds drove down the road as they spoke.

"You know Melissa, don't you think we've held this secret long enough from him? I mean the kid's nineteen now, I think this is time. He's becoming a man." said Simon.

"Now Simon, you know we've discussed this already. The boy is just too young still. As of right now, he's had to distance his friendship with Ryan, live in a rich home, he barely makes any new friends, and he barely makes conversation with Samantha. Telling him about what we do would just put more pressure on him. I don't want him stressing enough as it is."

"He's making progress. I think after his first semester is over, we should talk to him about it and maybe he can start coming along with us! That would be fun, right?" Mrs. Robbins was never pleased with her talks, but she managed to swim through them.

"Let's just see where we can get with all of this. I want him to be completely okay with this."

Perfection Is Key

Back at Ryan's house, Zander was getting a small snack from the kitchen. He headed back up with it as he began to speak with Ryan.

"Man, your mom makes the best PB and J sandwiches," he said while taking a huge bite. He suddenly noticed the laptop wide open and covered in sheets of information, and pages of Rampage High. Zander leaned closer to it as he squinted a bit.

"Are you still lurking through the stories?" Zander continued.

"Bro, what do you think? You got to let a gangster do his little business, alright?"

"Shut the hell up," said Zander as he pushed Ryan's head while laughing.

"So, check this out. Every generation of kids who live within this city has gone to this school looking like the most precious little beings, but it's not that they want to, they're forced to. Apparently every four years, there's a new line of the most cunning of students. The jocks for these years...are right here. They call themselves P3." The memories of these guys came flooding back to Zander's mind.

"Oh yeah, my new friend Alyssa told me about them. I ran into them in the bathroom on my first day there. It was a little tough."

"Did they touch you? Like my dad always says, once someone tries to test you, you punch them in the throat if you must!! You then start to step on their hands. You pin down their shoulders, then you start rip-"

"Ryan! Ryan! Bro, chill out. They didn't do anything to me."

"Well, did they say anything?"

"Nothing nice, that's for sure. Apparently one of them is the owner of the school along with the principal."

"Well, if they're going to hate so much, it's only cause they're staring at you. You don't have to play superman for those guys. But most of all, I would stay away from them."

"I've heard. So, what else do you know about these guys?"

Christopher Martinez

"Well... these three are the rulers of Rampage. They can be worse than scary, they are vicious. At least that's what the heading says. Apparently, they will literally bite off every little thing about you and turn it into something so worthless." Zander rolled his eyes.

"Gosh, this needs to stop. Maybe they're just misunderstood. Who knows what could have happened during their childhood, or what they could be dealing with at home? Either way, it needs to be exposed."

"Z, I don't mean to burst your bubble, but you can't really change it. Anyone who lives within the city reproduces with others in that damn city, the perfection you see daily, will continue to live on. I mean, it's like what you taught me. You can't force anything. People are going to be people. No matter what. You really need to just talk with your parents about moving elsewhere. The more you're there, the deeper you'll fall into the rabbit hole."

"Not with that attitude!" Zander said with a small chuckle. "Look man, I know I can't force anyone to change, but encouragement is still a weapon." Zander's face fell as he then lowered his head. His thoughts started taking over. He began overthinking everything. It was a main habit of his. He continued. "What if I'll never be accepted? What if P3 was right about me?"

Ryan could already tell what he was doing.

"That's just your insecurity. Don't let it attack you. I've always admired your strength and courage to the world. You make it seem calming, like everything was too shaken up, but you make it all steady again. YOU sir are a real inspiration."

"I'm sorry. I just never thought I would feel this way." Ryan nodded in agreement.

"We all have flaws. Everyone has gone through it. Some longer than others." Ryan then padded Zander's back as he swooped over to his laptop.

Perfection Is Key

"What are you doing?" asked Zander.

"I'm making sure these douchebags don't hurt my best friend! Look I was the muscle around you when you were here, and now that you're gone, I don't know...that's why I am going to hack this place, maybe find my way into connecting to their cameras and then I'll be able to see what I can do. I'll help you out with this exposure."

"This is why I honor you. You're a dangerous man, but a fun loser like me." They each laughed at each other.

Throughout the weekend, the boys were having the times of their lives. The days were getting closer to Monday and Zander needed to head back to Rampage. And when it came to playing football, Zander tried not getting hit in the face.

By Sunday, the two sat in the living room, playing Zander's favorite game, Mortal Kombat. Ryan's father walked in with a box of pizza.

"You guys hungry? I've got a whole box right here!"

"Dad, you know I can't eat too many carbs. We had eaten over at Burger King earlier, so now I've got to wait." Ryan replied.

"What? Since when did you start caring about your eating habits?" Ryan's father said as Ryan started laughing.

"I'm kidding. I can't even gain weight if I wanted to."

Zander's phone rang as he answered. His mother began to tell him that they would soon be leaving to go back home. He hung up as he turned his attention back to Ryan.

"Alright man, we have an hour before I leave. Do you think we have enough information to find more ways to report this place?" Ryan scanned faster through the reviews that he had.

"Okay, I forgot to tell you that I found their identities, and some information on that P3."

Christopher Martinez

Each of their faces popped up on the screen with a short summary lying right next to them. Zander leaned forward to the screen to read.

"James Coleman, a sixteen-year-old. He lives with filthy rich parents, he specializes in workouts, and his hobbies include football, debate, basketball, and being a ruler of Rampage," said Zander. "Liam Dixon, a fifteen-year-old. He grew up in a rich home, specializes with fashion, and his hobbies are football, modeling, fashion designing, and being a ruler as well."

"Sounds like a waste of time with these guys," said Ryan.

"Lastly, we have Dylan Anderson, a seventeen-year-old. He comes from a foster home, helps at his father's business, which is owning a mall. His hobbies include football, being spoiled, and just taunting literally everyone, even his own two wannabes. Wow, whoever wrote these were surely specific."

"If I were you, I would take heavy precautions. These three aren't really anything special, but as a human, and what they do, it seems like they could have more muscle over you, and by muscle, I mean power. Please, just don't get involved with them, and call me if anything happens, alright?" Zander felt his heart get warm. He nodded in agreement.

"Okay." The two clashed hands while ending with a hug. Zander now knew that this school wasn't going to be anything regular. His heart pumped so rapidly that he almost puked. Even though his fear was getting to his head, he knew he had a bunch of support along the way. Ryan noticed his worried face and padded his back.

"What's on your mind?" Zander stared at him.

"Nothing. I'll be fine. I was just thinking that...I'm really going to need a small upgrade just to look like I fit in. That way no more people bother me about it. I can at least LOOK like I fit in, and no one will ever know that those clothes will be just disguises to get through the day."

"Hmm. That is true. Why don't I buy you some clothes? I'm sure that once they notice your good looks, they won't even notice you anymore. They'll be too busy making sure no one else looks ugly or whatever. Eventually that will give us more time to finally report the behavior of the school and have it banished forever!"

"Ryan, I would say you're my hero, but wouldn't that ruin your money life? Buying one expensive piece of clothing would eat your wallet up."

"Bro, it's not about the money, that's what this world's about anyways. Everyone struggles with money. It's not a fun thing to have. Look, can you imagine coming across the largest party of the year and all the lights and eyes are now fixed on you because it's you? You'd make it all about the party. That's just what you need to do for now. Be perfect, and then take them down."

It had hit the last hour. Zander's bashful weekend had come to an end. He headed off to the car as his parents waited. Ryan had gotten some plans up his own sleeve, and his next move was going to be unexpecting for Zander. He shot out one last text message to him. Zander pulled out his phone.

Ryan: *Become a perfect member there just to stay in the school, we will get this school to be shut down, I promise. I will send the new clothes by tonight. How? I know a guy. In the meantime, good luck, and stay strong.*

Zander feared what might happen next. While sitting in the back of the car, he leaned over towards his parents and spoke.

"Hey, you guys wouldn't happen to know how to--" He then stared at his mother's cheek as it had three huge cuts gliding across it.

Christopher Martinez

"What happened to your face?" he continued.

"Oh, we came across your Aunt Jules, and you know me, I just had to play around with her cat," said Melissa. Her smile seemed too good to be true, but he didn't focus on it.

"Anyways, I have a question. What would you wear if you were trying to look handsome, or beautiful? Like as if you were going to go to a fancy ball dance, or something."

"Hmm, well I don't know. I would probably wear some nice makeup, and some expensive diamond jewelry," said Melissa.

"Honey, he's a dude," said Simon as he smirked at her.

"I know! I'm just saying maybe add some more accessories. Maybe even show some skin," she said with a raised eyebrow just to see what Simon would say. He scoffed at her. Zander leaned back as they continued driving. He began to think. After a few more minutes, the Robbins were back in the city of Rampage.

It was getting late, and Zander dug out some old boxes that his grandfather left behind. It held all kinds of gold and luscious items. He placed them all on his dresser as he then waited for the new clothes that Ryan had bought for his big plan. He stared out the window to see if anyone was near, but his mother knocked on the door and said the box was randomly delivered to him.

"Want to tell me what you ordered?" she asked while smiling at him. He stopped in his spot as he lowered the box.

"There are some things that I want to change about me. So, I got me some new clothes. Don't worry, Ryan helped."

"Well, why would you want to do that?"

"It's just a little complicated. I mean a new school, you know?"

"What about it? Honey, you don't have to change your appearance." She caressed his face as he smiled slightly at her.

"Have you seen these kids, mom? This isn't a normal city." She then leaned in and kissed his forehead.

Perfection Is Key

"Just be you," she said.
As she walked into the bedroom, Zander opened the box to find the most enticing clothing he had ever seen along with cologne, some shoes, and some hats. He set his new look upon the nightstand he had and was prepared for the next day. Time to play, Rampage.

Christopher Martinez

Chapter Four
King of The Jungle

As the weekend went on, Zander managed to prepare himself, to show the school that he too can look like a ken doll, yet on Monday, things got a little carried away.

At first, he was going to impress everyone with his new looks. He swung open the doors, and all eyes were glued to him. Their phones flashed like paparazzi, and he felt like the number one star on Broadway. He wore his hair back, the coolest shades sat in front of his eyes, chains hung so delicately around his neck, upon his wrists and pant loops too.

The gold layered with diamonds popped out the eyes of everyone. The piercings made his ears sparkle, and his shirt was so tight, it copied his shape. The leather jacket with spikes made him look like a rebel, it was just too shocking to see. The shiniest of all shoes, and his scent made all the girls want to kiss him. Alyssa walked up to him with a wide smile.

"Wow, I didn't think you had it in you. I am loving the chains and this killer leather," she said.

"Why thank you. I mean I had some help, but other than that, this feels amazing! This is going to be the only thing that can keep me in this school. I've got a plan. And it's going to be one for the books."

"Ooo, you sure got it all figured out, huh? You're starting to look like a real superstar now."

Behind the fake look, Zander felt like throwing up a bit, but he stuck with the idea of being a perfectionist for the plan of reporting the

Christopher Martinez

school to succeed. It was almost like being the male version of Hannah Montana. Two lives can be hard. Alyssa should know anyways.

It was lunch time, and Zander sped off to the bathroom to check up on his outfit. Little did he know, the top king of the school was in the same room. Zander jerked his jacket over his chest as he then sighed at his reflection.

A sudden crash sound of the stall door meeting the wall. Dylan Anderson was in the picture and there was no going back.

"Ahh, look who it is, it's the same little stick boy that came in on the first day! I see you've sort of improved your style." Zander freaked out at the sight of Dylan standing next to him.

"Uhm...I," he hesitated.

"Stop the stutter. Your appearance says enough. You know, I am flattered that you think you're cool now, but you're still not. No one ever stoops to my level." Dylan's ego struck out immediately. Zander's heart began to pound in his chest.

"I'm sorry, I just thought that-"

"Uh! No need for your pity." Dylan slowly began to stare him down. "You sure have some good features. I mean, not as great as mine, but you seem like a great experiment." His voice was so deep, it felt like talking to the President.

"Me? You want to help me become...popular?"

"Maybe some more tan and maybe whitened the teeth just a little more, then we could actually get somewhere." Zander felt scared, but he also felt the excitement nag at him to go along with everything. Dylan then brushed off his shoulders and positioned him toward the mirror.

"How would you like to be the next member in my group?"

Perfection Is Key

The thought and imaginations of being in P3 were a bit scary to think about, but at the same time, Zander's desire for the power was so strong. He kept the idea of exposing everything in front of his head. But adding this would make it a little more fun.

"Yes! Yes! I mean uhm...yeah," he replied with a geeky smile. Dylan smirked as he then put his arm around Zander. They walked out and into a random room that was meant only for Dylan. It was his hideout. Dylan sat him down. He then began to speak.

"Look, first things first, we need to change everything about you. One, there's no abs, two, you've got freckles, which no girl likes whatsoever, and three, you need to make it fresh!"

"Okay... make what fresh?" It had only been a minute, and Zander couldn't seem to control his desire. He was ready to act but wasn't thinking too much about what exactly he was getting himself into.

"Your personality. I've got an idea as to how you can get more people to be your friends and adore you. You got to have the swag." Dylan then stared at his watch as he sort of sighed.

"Crap. Uhm, look, I'm going to be right back, Liam wants me to try on this new suit that he bought for me. Stay here and don't touch anything." Zander nodded in agreement.

Just before Dylan could get to the door, a young girl was sitting down on the couch that was set in the back of the room. She stood up and walked over to him. Her brunette hair bounced a little as she strutted across the room. She wore an off-shoulder top, covered in dark maroon along with buttons lined up in the center. Her eyes were emerald deep blue. Her pants printed out her curves and she wore heels to complete her look. She was a bit intimidating.

"Uhm, hold up! I texted you like ten times, and you didn't answer. What's up with that?"

Christopher Martinez

"Sorry babe, I have a guest to take care of, as you can see. But I promise we'll go get your new nails later. Alright?" The two pecked each other's lips. She suddenly turned her attention to Zander. She walked over and took a seat next to him. Her flashy smile grew across her cheeks. Dylan stood off to the side as he watched the two very carefully.

"Hi. I don't believe we've met. I'm Miranda Stevens. And you are?" Her hand stood in midair, waiting for Zander to shake it.

"Uh, hi. Zander Robbins," he said as he then shook her hand. She let out a small laugh at his gazing, yet awkward smile.

"I guess you're joining P3?" she asked.

"Yeah. Dylan gave me the offer." Zander wasn't making much eye contact.

"A very rare offer." Dylan said while giving a wink at Zander. He then grabbed Zander by the arm. He rushed him over to a giant golden framed mirror.

Dylan was the king of the school. It was like his job to show newbies that they were a nobody until they became popular and pretty. Dylan shoved Zander close to the mirror.

"Whoa. What are you doing?" asked Zander.

"You know what I see in this mirror? I see a legendary young man with a large crowd of losers who'll bow down to him," said Dylan.

Zander gave an awkward smile as he just nodded and stared at his reflection. He began to imagine the whole idea. The whole city crowning him with a large crown and sitting by Dylan Anderson.

"Oh crap, I forgot you're still here." Dylan continued as he then laughed. "Listen, I'll be back with some material later. You can have a seat over there for now. And be sure that no one else walks in here. There's been enough dirt dragged in with you already."

Perfection Is Key

Dylan's smile seemed cruel to Zander as he headed out to find Liam. This left Zander in distress and hunger, but he did his best to ignore the pain.

"Well, I guess I'll head out too. Nice meeting you," said Miranda as she swooped her purse chain over her shoulder and headed out of the room.

He stared around the room. Its appearance and its portraits made it look like a magnificent mansion, or even an elegant lair. He then took a few minutes and stared at his own reflection once again. His thoughts began to crowd his mind once again.

"What am I? Some sort of rat? Gosh, I knew I shouldn't have got involved! I should've just run out of the room when I had the chance! But I mean, he's going to make me better. I can finally be on top of it all. It'll be a fun ride."

The bell suddenly rang, and everyone passed on by in the halls. Zander's heart began to race as he waited eagerly for Dylan to burst through the door. The suspense was killing him. He could feel the tears blazing his eyes. His phone suddenly buzzed in his pocket.

Alyssa: *Where are you?*

Zander: *In the king's lair.*

Alyssa: *What? As in Dylan's lair? I thought I warned you.*

Zander: *Relax. He wants me to join his group. But remember, I have a plan.*

Dylan strutted in with his crew as he tossed his champion football. There was a glare that made his eyes look dead. He lifted the ball in his hand as he hollered for Zander.

Christopher Martinez

"Hey Z! Catch!" Dylan threw the ball hard enough to knock Zander in the face. James and Liam laughed as they clashed hands with Dylan and pumped each other's chest. He walked up to him.

"Awe was that too hard of a throw?" he asked. He then wiped some blood off Zander's cheek. The embarrassment took over Zander's entire body.

"This is the nerd you're trying to make into one of us?" said James with a judging tone. He let out a laugh while staring down at Zander. Dylan straightened his back and let out a sigh.

"Relax. I know what I'm doing. And... why not add another member?" The tone in his voice made him sound like he didn't care, but at the same time, he sounded like he was wanting more power over everyone, especially by adding Zander to the group.

"Uhm, Dylan, I should head out. I've got a quiz that I need to take next period. How about I catch you guys later? Maybe after school?" said Zander while grabbing his backpack. Dylan stared at him for a moment.

"Alright, yeah man. I'll hit you up later."

As Zander began to walk down the hall, he felt as if a heavy rock was lifted off his shoulders. Alyssa walked up to his side.

"Good. You're still in one piece. Want to tell me what the heck just happened?" she asked.

"You'll never believe it. It was insane. He caught me in the bathroom and then we started talking. I mean, he was mainly telling me everything was wrong with me or whatever, and then he asked me to join his group. And it makes my plan even better."

"And what exactly is this plan of yours? Why do you even have a plan?"

"It's a personal thing for now. Look, I'm sure I'll be able to share it with you soon, but for now, just be my friend through it."

She then stared closely at his nose.

Perfection Is Key

"Whoa. What happened to your nose? Did he do that to you?"

"I'm fine. I promise. It was just Dylan's friendly teasing...I think."

"I don't know what you're getting yourself into, but if it gets too dangerous, you let me know, and I will get you out of it."

By the end of the day, Zander headed home. And throughout the evening, he told his parents about everything that had happened so far. And they were not happy about it. To hear about all the bullying made them worry about Zander. Though they couldn't do much with their spy mission getting in the way, they always tried their best to fight for him.

"Son, this doesn't sound too good. I think I should just go down there and talk with them about this situation. No one taunts my kid," said Simon.

"Uh, Simon, there's some other things that need to be taken care of, don't you think?" said Melissa with a secretive tone.

"Are you kidding? Our son's been falling into some tight traps, and you want us to focus on that?!"

"It begins in an hour," she responded demandingly.

"Fine," said Simon as he stared back at Zander. "Sorry son, your mother and I must go. We'll have to talk about this later, okay?"

"Don't worry sweetie, we'll be back to deal with this, okay?" Melissa said as she kissed Zander's cheek.

They both headed off in a rush.

Zander managed to deal with these issues a bit on his own. After all, there was nothing serious going on.

Later that night, Samantha had come to visit. And a few things almost slipped. She was a little uncareful with her words.

Christopher Martinez

"I'm sorry I didn't catch you today. I got caught up with some tests to bring up some grades. Mr. Adams doesn't like us to miss out on a lot of assignments. He's just a very strict teacher."

The two had been talking for a couple of hours, but Zander couldn't hold back all the questions in his head.

"Sam, please tell me how you are making it work here. I mean, how are you and your family still living here? Did you all protest for everyone to accept you?" he asked.

She lowered her head.

"What do you mean?"

"You dress normal, bring out the real you, and you seem to have no issues with anyone here. Are you sure you go to school here?"

She laughed at him.

"I just have my way around this city. Trust me, I've got my own struggles as well."

"You know what, forget it. I'm putting my trust in you because you're one of the people that I can depend on for now. I've got a plan to expose this place and get it shut down." He suddenly paused for a moment. "Oh yeah! I can even tell Alyssa! She's another friend of mine that I've met at school. Ahh this is going to be great!"

Samantha stood there with hesitation and a faint smile. She then played around with her bracelet as she looked a little pale.

"Zander, look I don't think we should get involved with trying to expose Rampage. These people are never going to listen to us. Plus, with P3 and Principal Shue, we'd be so screwed. I'm sorry, but this is not going to happen. I just can't go through with this."

"Are you kidding? This is our one chance where we could show what having freedom is about. Don't you want to be free? Just imagine chilling out on the beach, going out to the mall, or even out to a restaurant and there's no one there to judge you for not being some pretty thing." He pulled out his phone with excitement.

Perfection Is Key

"What are you doing?" she asked intensively.

"Calling Alyssa, we got to get her on this!" She quickly reached for his phone.

"No, no, Zander please, let's just leave it all alone."

The two were suddenly talking over each other until Samantha had slapped his phone out of his hand. He looked at her with a glare. Silence filled the room for a moment. The phone chimed once more.

Unknown: *What up Z! Ready to take the next move in popularity? Meet me at my place, 6:30 sharp! 1655 Ave D!*

He smirked. He knew it was Dylan. 'Z' had become Zander's nickname for Dylan.

For the plan to work, he had schemes of getting along with P3 until he could finally reveal that they were the losers, finally kill their ego, and get the school to be shut down forever.

In the meantime, Ryan went home after school and after days of practice as he stalked up the pages and information on Rampage and its people. He had gained access to the Anderson's household.

Dylan's house was a three story one, so it was hard keeping track of almost every room there was. It was funny that only three people lived there. I guess to show that he was quote unquote "King of the Jungle."

Ryan then put in his earbuds and activated the microphone. The first camera zoomed in on the living room. He and Zander were on the hunt. To start the spark was Dylan.

A loud knock on the door and Dylan opened it wide.

"Zander! My boy, thanks for the lovely visit! Come on in!" His parents stood aside with shining smiles, though you could tell they

Christopher Martinez

were fake. They wore the tightest clothes with their hair styled in pounds of grease and hairspray. Standing almost as if he were face to face with some sort of serial killer.

Zander wore one of his new looks to impress the family. Gold, shiny bracelets, shiny shoes, hair pulled back, heavy chains around the neck, and rings. His leather jacket shot out his ego.

"These are my foster parents. Guys, this is my new buddy, Zander Robbins. He's the one I'm including in my group. He and his family are new in town. Nothing special."

"Mm, well it's nice to meet you," said Mrs. Anderson as she tried to blossom her smile.

"You too. You guys have a very lovely home," said Zander with a small crack.

"Well, let it smother you. Just remind me to dust off everything he touches," said Mr. Anderson as he and his wife laughed viciously. To be someone who loved pointing out the little things about Zander was always an insult to him.

"Alright, can y'all shut up? We've got some work to do, so stay down here where you won't embarrass me. Not after what happened last time," said Dylan.

Zander turned his head to ignore the awkwardness, and his eyes became glued to Miranda, who seemed to walk straight out of Dylan's Kitchen, she flashed a bright smile.

"Oh hi! Zander, isn't it? I remember anyone's face."

After waving his hand at her, he turned his attention away. Dylan grabbed her hand as he pulled her close to him.

"Hey baby, gosh I've missed you so much. And you look so beautiful. Hey, did your mom get to buy all the things she needed?"

"Yeah, at least for today. I doubt that she'll get anything next time. Maybe help a little?" she asked with a pouting look, yet she batted her eyes.

Perfection Is Key

"Maybe. I need the restroom. Be right back, okay? Stay put Z." Zander just nodded, feeling like he was respecting some sort of sergeant on a military base. He was so nervous, he almost barfed up his lunch.

After a few seconds, Zander sat in the living room along with Miranda. She looked him up and down then suddenly sat right beside him. She crossed her legs as she giggled a little.

"So, do you like it here in Rampage?" She slid her hands down her lap to smoothen out her skirt.

"I guess. I mean, after Dylan's offer, I think I can get real used to it. Though sometimes, I think it's kind of over the top. Not to sound rude or anything of course."

"No, I get that. But it's not that bad. Soon, you'll have the whole city adoring you as well. I mean, you're already sexy enough." She suddenly began to slide her hand across his back as his eyes widened a little.

"Uh, not really, but I think it'll definitely get to that point," he said as he scooted over.

"It's okay. You're really going to dazzle this city. All the girls are going to go crazy over you. I know I have." Zander felt a bit uncomfortable. Miranda seemed to have many tricks up her sleeve. Every time Zander would see her, she would always try to show her breasts more than usual. It was always sort of a sexual tease.

"Uhm, yeah, well, Dylan's king after all. I'm sure that's why you chose him," he said with an awkward laugh.

Dylan yanked open the door as he spotted Miranda playing with Zander's hair.

"Yo, what's going on here?" They both stood up as Miranda snuck a small paper into Zander's back pocket. He looked so pale, he almost wanted to push her away and run upstairs.

Christopher Martinez

"Oh nothing, just welcoming our new friend here," she said. Zander gestured towards him to go up to his room.

"Alright, well, let's go ahead and get started," said Dylan.

As they walked up the stairs, Zander began to speak softly into his earpiece.

"I'm really nervous."

"Just keep going, we'll see what he does. And what was up with his girl gaining all up on you? That was weird," said Ryan as he watched carefully. He then switched to the camera hanging in Dylan's bedroom.

"How exactly did you manage to get these cameras in here?" continued Zander in a whispering tone.

"I know a girl who would do anything for me, and I mean anything. Funny story, you know, one time we hung out at this bar, and after about ten drinks, we both snuck out to the bathroom, stripped only our shirts off, then she unbuckled my pants-"

"Ryan, focus." Ryan shook his head while clearing his throat.

"Sorry," he said.

Dylan opened two fancy doors that revealed a large room. Zander couldn't believe what he was seeing. The painted walls were covered in gold and silver, posters of him in modeling careers, idols, and famous football players. The bed was huge with a frame of royalty. *Perfection Is Key* was imprinted across it.

The dresser was tall and stood elegantly with three large mirrors standing on top of it. They were enticing and thick. Like 3D figures. His colognes and accessories lied perfectly organized on top. His closet was filled with very rich clothing.

"Gee, some room you got here," said Zander.

"Yeah, my parents used to sleep in this one, but I wanted it, so I took it for myself." He threw his backpack onto the bed as he pulled out the chair by his little desk.

Perfection Is Key

"Hm. So what are we doing exactly?"

"Making you another backup, remember? We need to start with a whole new you." Zander thought for a moment.

"Okay, like what?" Ryan's eyes grew wide as he continued watching. "It won't be anything painful, right?" continued Zander.

"Are you that much of an idiot? You want to fit in, right? Then trust me and let me work my magic. Otherwise, you can go back to being a member of the crowd. You can kiss my foot every morning."

"C'mon, you don't really think I need that, do you?" Dylan carried a pill in one hand and a bottle of some black liquid in the other.

"Oh, so drugs."

"No, I'm not a crackhead. I'm the finest man alive. This little bad boy is a pill that'll make your muscles and tissue thicken just a bit, that way you'll have some meat on your body. Everyone loves a man with the right amount of body fat. Though, you could probably get with James about that. Anyways, then you'll drink this liquid to boost your veins."

"What? That seems dangerous." The liquid was pitch black; it was almost like looking at a cup of squashed bugs.

"You don't want to be a stick the rest of your life, do you?"

"Bro c'mon, you know that isn't the case. I just think-"

"Shut up and take the damn pill." Dylan's face became serious. The tone in his voice was demanding.

Within a second, Dylan shoved Zander to the ground and made him swallow the pill and drink the liquid after. Zander tried fighting him through it, but there was no use. Dylan had a lot more strength. For a moment, everything stopped. Zander lied on the floor while trying to recover his breathing.

Ryan grew angry at the sight of what was happening. He was sort of hollering from the other side of the screen.

"C'mon bro, get up!"

Christopher Martinez

"Alright! Good boy, it's done. Now, time for some real fun. The injection," said Dylan with his victory voice. He came to his feet as Zander continued lying on the floor, holding his chest. He began to try and lift himself back up.

"Whoa, injection? Aren't you going a little too far?" Zander asked.

"Of course not. I did it to James and Liam and they're fine with it! That's what made them the men that they are today!"

"Well for all I know, you probably could've put some controlling spell on them." Dylan scoffed at him.

"I guess you could put it like that, but ay, they're popular and they wouldn't change a single thing about it all." He winked at him as Zander became disgusted at his sight.

"Now sit still." He grabbed his arm until Zander pulled it away.

"Wait, what exactly is this going to do?"

"Don't worry about that. Your life's about to change into an idolized one. You can thank me later for it." Dylan grabbed a magazine and slapped it onto Zander's lap. The cover was overfilled with models.

"Here, go through it and take a good look at how these models work. You see how they're special and perfect? I mean, wake up and smell the reality man! No one's going to waste a single rose on your heart!"

While Dylan taunted Zander about the models, he quickly injected him. Unfortunately, Zander couldn't feel a thing due to his mind being overshadowed by insecurity and hate. His own envious thoughts had crumpled his heart already.

"Alright, just do it quickly!" Zander screamed while tightening his eyes shut.

"It's already done bro. You're now ready to become a perfect guy. Like me, only I'm the best of the best."

Perfection Is Key

"You're delusional. The stuff you're doing doesn't make the world yours."

"But you see, now that I am in this world, I own the damn place! Look in that mirror and tell me something you see! Cause I see nothing." The room felt like a large ball of heat was sitting in the center of it.

"I see me. Look man, I'm grateful for this offer, but there's nothing wrong with me."

Arguing with a lion caused mighty roars. Dylan clenched a fist and slammed it onto the mirror, causing shards to fall and leaving a hole in the middle of the spot.

"GODDAMMIT! You see, this is why Mr. Shue put me in charge of taking care of shitty people like you! I hate it when everyone thinks they can just do whatever they want! This is my fucking town! My home!! And I don't need little bitches like you coming in here and ruining this shit!! Being ugly is not a choice! When you're born like that, that's how you are! There can never be takebacks because you sir will never be anything! You are not enough!" He swung his hand across his little desk, knocking off a few belongings.

Zander felt his fear rise to his throat as Dylan then covered his bloody fist. Zander was ready to burst into tears. Little did he remember; Ryan was keeping track of the cameras and had grown in anger at how Dylan was treating his best friend. He had never liked seeing him in pain or suffering.

After a few weeks, Zander Robbins was no longer the same kind, caring boy that everyone once knew. He was officially perfect. His parents felt like there were days where they couldn't recognize Zander. Popularity grew around him.

Ryan on the other hand was upset that his own best friend was slowly, but surely removing him from his life. Rare communications and less contact. Their friendship was crashing. Even though Ryan had

Christopher Martinez

never let anything small mess up his mentality, losing his best friend made everything feel like there were constant fires and riots.

Another day at Rampage High and Zander was officially one of the school's biggest jerks. He became apathetic. A rebellious jock in the halls. His pride shot higher each day. While walking down the hall, a young woman stopped him.

"Hey there young man, can you tell me where I can find room 203? I have a meeting with Mr. Mendoza about some paperwork with the Police Station." He gave a snarl at her as he swooped his leather jacket over his chest.

"Do I look like some sort of map or something? It's not that great of a school. Keep walking missy." Before he could get any further, the woman stopped him once more.

"Excuse you sir, but this is urgent, can you just try and tell me which hallway he's in? It won't be much of a bother." Zander stopped in his steps and turned his head.

"Ugh, gosh lady! Just go straight down the hall! Be careful with those wolves though, little red!" The woman stayed quiet as she adjusted her vest. She turned her attention away as she began to walk down the hall.

Alyssa had her secrets. One day, she chatted with Dylan and Mr. Shue in the office. She began to have a small rant. Yet she knew how to stand her ground. She began to pace the floor.

"Why can't you both get your heads straight and turn Zander back the way he was!? He probably didn't want to take the offer in the first place. Making him become an ass like your own drone here doesn't make any sense."

"What exactly do you know about this Zander Robbins? Miss Reed, we have a strict policy here and it's as simple as it gets. Zander Robbins is the new kid. We do it to every new kid because our school is all about perfection. You should know that by now. You don't want to have us bring back the old routine again. Do you?" asked Principal Shue as he placed his fingertips against each other and stared deviously at Alyssa. Dylan cocked his head to the side as he scoffed at their words.

"I mean what's so wrong with being perfect and wanting others to be?" he asked. "This is the kind of world that everyone wants! I am a god here! No one will ever change that."

"It's stupid! Nothing good comes from forcing others to be a copy of your damn self! Not everyone is you, Dylan!" Dylan and Mr. Shue smirked at each other.

"Go ahead Miss Reed...continue. Either way, you know you have no power to control anything here! You're just as low as everyone else." The two had known her before and seemed to have some terrible history with her as well. As they tickled a tease at her, she sat back down and pouted as Dylan sat up.

"Remember we created you," said Dylan. She sat in eagerness to run, but she had nowhere to hide. She felt lost.

Ryan was a complete mess without his best friend. Due to his overwhelming thoughts, he started messing up with grades, sports, and even daily life duties. He was a straight A student, of course, but each one dropped to an F in a matter of seconds. He was the most skilled in football until they lost two games, and all he could think about was revenge on P3. His coach could tell something was wrong

Christopher Martinez

from the moment it all began. One day after practice, Coach Reyes walked over to Ryan.

"Hey kid, you know whatever's bothering you, you can speak about it with me, or any of us coaches. A real man never hides away in his feelings," he said while taking a sip from his small coffee cup. Ryan stood by his opened locker.

"Thanks Coach, but it would be something I would discuss with my best friend. It just sucks cause he's not talking to me right now. At least not as much as I would want. Things have gotten a little complicated."

"Well, we've all been through the stage of frenemies, but everything will come back around. No true friend let's something small get in the way of a real friendship." Ryan changed his shirt and packed up everything in his locker.

"Yeah? Do you ever mess up something so bad that it feels like there's no solution to it?"

"Kid, mistakes make life the roller coaster ride. Without them, where's the preaching and fun of destroying evil?"

"I hope he sees it that way. At least, someday."

"If he has your faith and support, he'll come back around. You're a great student. I know you'll make it through this." Ryan felt a small boost of support and swung his bag over his shoulder.

"Thanks Coach! I might just try and talk to him." In confidence, Ryan drove on home. He had enough hope for Zander. He was going to make sure Zander remembered who he was. No matter the risks and challenges.

Chapter Five
They Admire the Body

It was officially Homecoming Week. The excitement was over the top. And even though perfection colored the walls of the school, everyone still dressed up as if it were a gala. But this meant more than being crowned king or queen. They were labeled 'Legends,' and 'Gods,' and 'Majesties.'

Zander had spent the night at Dylan's house. James and Liam sat around in Dylan's room as they spoke about the Homecoming dance. But their conversation wasn't normal, obviously.

"Who do you think's going to win Legend?" asked James as he flexed his arm in the huge mirror that stood in front of him.

"Dylan. What kind of question is that? He's always won," said Liam who was also busy comparing two different colored patterned pieces of cloth.

"Remember when he had the whole school staff double their voting on him last year?" asked James.

"That was hilarious! Their scared little faces," said Liam with a menacing laugh.

Zander rushed into the room. He peeked at his phone as he began to search the place.

"Wow, I just realize that Dylan's winning on his third year! Homecoming Legend once again," continued James.

"Homecoming Legend?" asked Zander as he stopped.

Christopher Martinez

"Yeah! You see, first we start off as kings, then you get bumped up to Legend on Homecoming," said James as he slapped his hands onto Zander's shoulders.

"And prom is Prom God or Goddess," continued Liam. Zander felt confused as he tried to understand the whole meaning behind everything.

"Okay?" said Zander with a confused look.

He then walked around the room and continued searching. He was opening drawers and moving things over on shelves. He took a small breath and placed his hands on his hips.

James took a good look at Zander. His eyes stared him down as he scanned his body. Who knew what all was going through his mind? But whatever it was, it didn't seem good. Liam interrupted his train of thought.

"What are you looking for?" asked Liam.

"There's this thing that Dylan asked for. He said it was a very shiny-"

James reached into his pocket and pulled out a small box.

"Lucky charm," he said with a blank, yet annoyed face.

"Yes, thanks. Wait, why do you have it?"

"I carry it with me because I'm the keeper of it. Which is why I'm wondering why he didn't ask me to bring it to him."

"Oh, I don't know. He just told me to get it." Dylan hollered from downstairs as Zander rushed out. James wasn't pleased with what just happened but was more focused on how Zander looked.

He took a seat on the edge of the bed and Liam scrolled through his phone.

"Bro, did you notice how skinny Zander looked?"

"What do you mean?"

"He's too skinny. Like, the swag is great like Dylan's, and his skin became perfectly tan like his too, but his body is so...bony."

Perfection Is Key

"Well, first off, his outfit looking like Dylan's is nothing compared to my kind of style. Second, he is okay. If he looks perfect, there's nothing to worry about."

James flexed his arms, and his muscles grew making him look buff. They were of course, not too big, nor too small, they were just simply perfect.

"Ahh. I see," said Liam as the two smirked.

"Yeah, you see where I'm getting at?"

"Yeah. I mean, he is a new member, if he wants to stay, he's got to finish the track of pain." James smirked at him as he grabbed his phone and began to open random apps.

James had schemed the next level of perfection. All he had to do now was chisel him out.

Zander had finally come back home after what felt like an exhausting day. He walked in with a tired face. His father sat on the couch with a book on his lap and a laptop on the other. He glanced up at Zander and smiled.

"Hey bud! How was school today? Did you score any new friends or maybe even some lovers?"

"Uh, no. Just another boring day filled with lots of work. Listen, I'm going to be in my room, so don't bother me."

Before he could get any farther, his mother stopped in front of him.

"Uh no sir. We are about to start dinner. C'mon, sit with your father and help him with his work for a bit. I just need to make some more side veggies and finish up the punch, and we'll be all set."

"Well, I'm sure Dad's going to be alright. All you need is to maybe slap those idiots and speak the truth. Your boss can't always be

Christopher Martinez

in control of what you do. It's best to take up your own road," said Zander.

His parents' face dropped. They exchanged a look with each other. How else do you react when you see someone you love turn into a snobby person?

"Zandy." Melissa said nervously.

"Don't call me Zandy! I was five at the time. I'm a man now. I don't need my parents calling me baby names. Maybe it's you guys that need to learn how to grow up."

"Now Zander. You know we don't use that tone." He came close to his mother with a deadly look in his eyes.

"Oh I'm sorry this seems to be more about you." He scoffed. "Trust me, once I get a tone, you sure as hell wouldn't want to hear it."

"Zander Robbins, you do not use that tone with your mother!" yelled Simon. Zander turned his face towards him. He then took a slow, deep breath.

"Ugh, you people irritate me!!"

Melissa held on to Simon as they each stared at him while he walked angrily up to his room. She then stared at Simon.

"We should talk to Samantha and her family. Maybe they can help us with him. Zander's letting all this luxury get to his head. Maybe they can help him to remember what all this stuff can do," she said.

"You're right. Better that than me whipping him up with a few of my gadgets," said Simon.

Mr. & Mrs. Robbins sat in the Shaw's house as they spoke with Samantha and her parents about Zander's behavior.

"I don't understand. I thought Zander was someone different. He made that pretty clear when he first arrived. I don't understand why he's acting like this," said Samantha.

Perfection Is Key

"He's locked his own best friend out of his life," said Simon.

"Ryan?" asked Sam. "That's horrible. Zander told me so many great things about him. They're like crazy best friends."

"Yeah, well, things have turned ever since. We figured that maybe it had to do with some of the people he's been around lately. Like those new friends of his…uhm, what were their names?" Melissa said as she trailed off.

"P3 is the main center of the school," said Samantha. "I'll bet that he's let them get to his head. Especially if he's gotten any closer with Dylan. He's the worst of them all."

"Well, I can't let my baby boy get corrupted by popularity. I had a small phase of it when I was in high school, so I know what it costs," said Melissa.

"Oh, I know. Trust me, my high school career was like a horror show. There were too many crimes and dangerous events. My friends and I almost ended up in jail once," said Mrs. Shaw.

"Well, no worries. Zander is not going to help them grow. We'll get him out of this," added Samantha.

It had been a couple of hours, and the Robbins and Samantha headed over back to the house to try and talk some sense into Zander, but as they took their first step, a loud racket slithered against their ears. The house was shining with lights and filled with rowdy music.

Ryan had driven up to the edge of the curb at the right moment. He popped out of his car and began to walk up to the group. They each stood at the door, screaming and demanding for Zander to open it. Dylan caught sight of them through the window. He opened the door as he sighed heavily.

"Oh. You guys. You know, in case you haven't realized, Zander's trying to have a good time right now," he said.

Christopher Martinez

"Excuse me, but who are you? I am his mother and I demand you guys leave this house! You have no right taking over this place!" Melissa said.

"Dylan Anderson," he said with a boastful smile. "No pictures please. It's not a good time in case you haven't noticed." Dylan gestured towards the party. Ryan looked over his shoulder and searched for Zander.

"Zander! It's me, Ryan! Are you in there?! We really need to talk to you."

"Ooo best friend huh?" Dylan said as he stared at him up and down.

"Yeah, what's it to you? You're the punk who ruined him!"

"Mm. Did I though? Look around here. Looks like Zander's true friends came through for him and made him a whole lot better."

Samantha sighed and grew angry.

"Dylan, just get your head out of your ass for once and realize you're a big nothing like everyone else!"

"And you are?" he asked with a nasty glare.

"Not important. Just let us talk to Zander."

"Oh no sweetheart. I don't think Zander wants any visitors right now. In fact, it just be better if you all found a ditch and fell deep into it. Zander has a better life now and he sure doesn't need some slimy leaches like you. I mean, open your eyes! He found a new place to escape and doesn't need mommy and daddy anymore. He threw a party and didn't invite any of you."

"Now you listen here, young man, I don't think I appreciate you doing the things you're doing to my son. I suggest that you no longer speak to him. You and your little bratty friends need to pack up and get the hell up out of my house!" Simon insisted.

"Or what? You'll hit me with another *scary* little threat? I can get you people removed from this city and it won't just be packing up bags of clothes." Dylan's glare had Samantha's heart pumping. Ryan's anger was boiling, and Melissa almost felt a little too intimidated. Simon was no one to back down.

"Oh, trust me, boy. I could do a lot worse to you," he said.

Dylan never took threats seriously. He slammed the door and smirked. Having other people be put down and ignored was a big satisfaction for Dylan.

After the party was over, the Robbins had finally made it into their home. Ryan managed to spend the night to get a good conversation with Zander. His parents were furious. So, they ignored him in disappointment.

Zander ran downstairs and headed toward the kitchen. Simon, Melissa, and Ryan were having dinner. He stared at them for a moment.

"Is something wrong, son?" asked Simon.

"Since when was dinner served? I was upstairs for an hour. What, calling is too much now?" he asked in an aggressive tone.

"Oh, well, you were too busy with your friends and partying, that we kind of figured you'd feed yourself. You've shown us enough that you're a mature adult, right?" Zander scoffed.

"You guys are crazy. Let me get my plate. Oh, and welcome to Rampage bro," said Zander as he patted Ryan on the back. "I see you've dropped by. But if I were you, I'd leave as soon as morning hits. Looking like you would cause chaos in this city. I tell you, it's like living in Paradise. Everything is just perfect here. I think your cousin Jack was probably a nobody here." Ryan lifted a brow.

"Funny. Last time I checked, you were once a basic. We both had this promise when we were kids that no matter what, we were going to be okay with ourselves and that no one would ever take our

Christopher Martinez

places. We had our family, each other, the amazing neighborhood. Now look at you! You're being consumed by all this arrogance. It's making you break everyone who loves you."

Melissa sat in an awkward position as she picked at her food with her fork. If only she could slap her son silly and tell the two boys to stop bickering. But the conversation continued.

"Calm down. You make it sound like it's a bad thing! Dylan has shown me why I'm always wishing for the best of everything. He's helped me see what we're missing out on man! I could honestly hook you up with a meeting with him. He can give you some awesome tips."

Ryan scoffed with an annoying chuckle. He picked up his plate and shattered it against the wall.

"And that's exactly how you're going to end up if you keep it up with this little magic show of yours!" Ryan spat.

"Yo! What the hell's your problem?!" Zander spat back while coming to his feet.

"My problem? The problem here is that you've become a jerk! I thought the guy that I knew didn't care about little things like this! I thought he was more mature. Nice to the elderly's and caring for every single person on this planet! You need to get out of your big head man! It'll only lead you to your downfall. And you know it."

This took full offense to Zander. Only because he knew it was the truth.

"Nah man, this place needs me! They honor me!! Don't you know what that feels like!? It feels like you have the world and there is no one left to try and take it all away! For my entire life, *I* had nothing!!" Ryan breathed slowly.

"Wow. So, all those years of laying out to watch the fireworks, playing hoops with the guys, walking the park with a couple of cute girls... talking about all the troubles in our lives that we felt like we couldn't face. I guess that all meant nothing. And now it's all burned and erased." He gave a smile to Simon and Melissa. "Thank you so much for dinner, but I think I'll be heading home now. Let me know when the real Zander comes home." He turned his attention towards Zander. "Because this may look like my buddy, but you sure as hell are not him." Zander knew he felt his heart sort of shatter, but he kept his pride front and center.

Ryan then grabbed his jacket and yanked the door open. There was nothing left to say from him. Melissa finished her plate as she lowered her head and stood up. Tears began to stream down her face.

"Mom, c'mon don't cry. He's just being a hater. It's not his fault his parents made him a jackass." His father also stood up and fixed his tie. He then grabbed his wife and stared at Zander.

"I think we've seen enough of you tonight, son. Goodnight," said Simon.

Zander felt lost. He had no one to support him, but overall, he had no care. His phone buzzed on the edge of the table. He received a message from James.

James: *Hey man, come outside. We're taking a little trip.*

It had become midnight and Zander would be in bed by ten. But unfortunately, he saw time as just numbers and pulled all-nighters. He walked out and spotted James in his shiny ride. Before he got any closer, he noticed another person sitting in the car.

"Hey there little man! This is my girlfriend, Kristal. She's captain of the cheer squad. You may have noticed her around."

Zander shook her hand as he felt this spark sizzle through his body.

"Oh yeah, I think I've seen you. Everyone says you're like the best of the best."

Christopher Martinez

She was wearing a shirt covered in a pink and purple x pattern, her pants were folded halfway up her leg, and a small black coat over. Her smile was charming, as her hair was straight and brown. She was almost too stunning.

Zander gained control and he crawled into the backseat. James began to drive away, and they headed to his house. As James was beginning to pull onto another highway, the engine blew out. James got a bit upset and he checked for the issue.

Meanwhile, Zander and Kristal sat in silence for about two minutes. Then she spoke.

"So, I see you've made some improvements to your status. Becoming a member of P3 is quite the step up. I'm sure it's a crazy change, but I'll bet you're all over the place now."

"Well, don't want to brag, but…" She laughed at him.

"You're cute. I wonder… are you any good at math?" She rested her chin on her hand.

"Not really. Math has never been my subject. I am good with literature and reading and even English."

"Oh nice. Most of my mom's side of the family is good with all of that too. So then…is there anything else you're good at?" she asked while then sliding her hand slowly up and down his arm. He gave an awkward smile as he moved his arm away. She shot him another look. A very cunning look.

"Look I'm not okay with this. You got your boyfriend right there. I mean, he's fixing the car as we speak."

"He doesn't need to know. I mean, what world do you think we live in?" In a quick snap, James tapped on the window as Zander jumped in his seat. He rolled it down.

"Shit you scared me!" he said.

"Sorry man, but hey, see if you can give me that screwdriver on the floor there."

Perfection Is Key

As Zander handed him the tool, Kristal rolled her eyes. He rolled the window back up as he stared around the interior of the car. He began to feel his nerves twiddle.

"Well, that was too close. Maybe next time," she said while pecking her lips towards him.

James finally got the car to start again. And after an hour, Kristal was dropped off and the boys were onto the next level. At least James was.

"Nice place," said Zander as he walked into the house with an amazed face.

"Thanks. It's kind of ancient, but we like to keep it fresh."

"Uhm, so what exactly are we doing?"

The two stepped into a large, spaced room full of large and small sized workout equipment. Zander sort of stared around.

"This is our workout room and now that you are more like Dylan, it's time we fix up your body. Make it toned and fit."

"For real? I don't really think I can do that."

"Nah man, you definitely can, and you need it. You'll look great, I promise. They admire the body." Zander was intrigued and agreed to it all. He needed the body anyway, and he intended to get it.

"Alright then, let's do it," said Zander with a smirk.

"That's what I'm talking about!"

Zander went month after month, and day by day trying his best to improve his health. His diet meals made him miss burgers and hot dogs like crazy, but he knew better than to wish for any of it.

Eventually, Zander's body was becoming stronger. His abs barely popped out and his pecs were becoming more fit. His arms grew a bit as well. Then came a day where James insisted on doing an intense ab and leg workout. The rocking music blasted through the

Christopher Martinez

speakers in the background as they each kept the workout routine going.

"C'mon man, you have ten more reps to do! Don't give up on me now! You got this! Burns so good and feels so good! You got to tell yourself it does," said James.

Zander's breath was so heavy, he ended up stopping when there were five more reps to do. As he dropped onto the floor, James paused the music and stepped on over. His small, soaked towel wrapped around his neck.

"Whoa there. What are you doing?" he asked.

"Just resting man. That new workout is tough on me. Damn, who knew that it would be this tough on your muscles."

"It's supposed to be. Now c'mon, you can't just take breaks. You have to feel the power!"

Zander continued drinking his water.

"In a minute man. I really got to get a quick rest." James kicked the bottle out of his hands. He picked him up and practically threw him across the room.

"When it's time to work, we work," he said. His face was like staring at a toned out, too-strong-for-you type of wrestler. Zander felt a little unsafe, but what could he do? He was intimidated by the second power of P3.

"C'mon man...just a small-"

"Okay what the hell is the matter with you? Don't you get it? This is not even the hardest thing we've done, and you want to rest? You're not going to attract anyone with a face of weakness! You're never going to get hot chicks sitting all around you! You'll never be a part of this group if you're someone who gives up!! Now get your butt up and let's do this shit!" Zander felt a bit pissed off, but he tried catching more of his breath.

Perfection Is Key

James was always shirtless; it was just another thing that would make Zander want more for his body. He wanted to be fit just like James, so it meant that he would do his all.

"Okay...I'll do it! I mean you're right. Why rest? I need this body." The more Zander exercised, the more built he became.

A whole month had passed by and Zander was as fit and perfect as all the guys. He would walk the halls and all the girls would seduce him or drool over him. P3 was a new updated crew. Although it's still one of the meanest crews out there. Rampage High was still not complete for Zander though. There was still one more stage to go through.

Christopher Martinez

Chapter Six
Fashion Is My Kryptonite

Zander Robbins had become a new member walking behind Dylan's back. He dressed so perfectly like Dylan and became perfectly fit just like James. But P3 still had a third member. Liam Dixon. The most fashionable man you could ever see. Everyone in Rampage was stunning, but Liam was the master at it. Fashion was his go-to and his greatest skill.

And Zander looked great, but Liam had other plans for him. The boys gathered at Liam's house planning on how they were going to dress for Homecoming.

"I got it! What if you make my coat shiny black with a white design pattern on it?" asked James as he started to imagine himself in it.

"And make sure my clothes fit me tightly," said Dylan.

"Fellas. Chill out. I can make you look like the fanciest gods that walk in that gym. Have you not paid attention to my work over these past few years?" He popped his collar in pride.

The whole school reached out to Liam every year for a very fancy suit or dress. And they would pay him grands. He suddenly looked over at Zander.

"Yo, Z. I've been needing to tell you that you're nominated for Homecoming Legend," said Liam.

"Oh, really? Wow. Thanks for the info."

"Which is why I got to fix up your style."

"What? He already has a good style," said Dylan.

Christopher Martinez

"I mean, yeah, but he needs more god-like fashion. I made it work for all of us, didn't I?"

Zander stared down at his own outfit. Wondering what else could make him stand out in a crowd.

"It's just a dance. If I look handsome and nice, I'll be alright. Isn't that what it's all about?" asked Zander.

"Nah man. You need to make yourself look the most elegant. That's just a rule that runs on the list. You don't do it, then you're out of the group, for good," said Liam.

"Oh c'mon. I've already dealt with enough, aren't I perfectly perfect? I mean the school loves me now! The girls are all over me, and plus, Mr. Nickels gave me an A on a quiz I never even took. I mean how amazing is that?!"

"Not much."

Zander was being pressured enough with all the steps the boys were making him attempt. Along with Homecoming, everything just had to be perfect.

Liam pulled Zander over to the corner of his room where he would measure anyone who wanted to buy something from him and see what he could do to 'upgrade their style.' Meanwhile, Dylan and James discussed disturbing, yet non-surprising things about their girlfriends.

"Damn, Kristal asked me to be a part of her screwing game after the dance already," said James with a giant smile as if he'd just won tickets to a Super Bowl game.

"Ayyyyeee bro same! Miranda wanted to try new things. I don't see what else there is to try. We've tried almost every position. In fact, two days ago, after we left the bar, made her go up to four rounds." They both laughed as they felt proud and ignorant. Zander felt so uncomfortable.

Perfection Is Key

"Fuck yeah! I'm thinking we might get a little crazier than usual. Kristal has a kink for almost any little thing." They clashed hands and laughed. Zander gave a quick disturbed face as Liam chuckled at them.

"Hey, what about you Z? Any girls want to get it with you?" Liam asked while stitching through a small sleeve.

"Yeah bro, tell us!" said Dylan with his head held up a little, showing his jawline along with a small smirk.

"I bet they're all over you. Like I said, it's all about the body," said James. Zander felt a bit uneasy and felt the confidence to speak his truth.

"Well, I mean yeah, I've had a few ask me to the dance...but not get something out of it." He stood in silence for a moment. The boys stared around at each other with a confused look.

"Wait, don't tell us you've never done it," said Dylan as his expression formed like it was saying 'you're such a loser.'

"You're a virgin?" asked Liam.

"Yeah. Is that bad?"

They all stared at each other for another moment. Then it happened. They burst out in laughter. Zander felt humiliated and ashamed. Once again, he felt so much like an outcast.

"Dude, that is embarrassing!" Dylan exclaimed.

"What? No, it's not. It's not wrong to put in good timing."

"Right! Awe man, you want to be a legend, right? Get laid after the dance! It's worth it, I promise," said Dylan sarcastically yet with a daring deadly stare. Zander's face dropped. He stared in shock. His stomach began to twist.

"But dude...I can't do that. I promised myself and committed to waiting till it was time," said Zander. Poor guy didn't even realize that it was the one thing that young men feel is what makes you more masculine.

Christopher Martinez

"Okay. Then we'll go to option b. You rape someone," continued Dylan. Was he serious? Zander wanted to run out of there and never show his face ever again. Maybe doing everything he's done so far was all a mistake.

"Bro, calm down..." Zander knew the more he rejected, he would have a battle to deal with, so he thought quickly and made up a story. "HA! Fooled you all! I just said that cause I thought it was embarrassing to admit it. But I have done it. I'm just fucking with you bro." The lies were like snakes slithering out of his mouth.

"Ahh, I knew my homie was just messing with us!" said James.

"Yeah, it was back in seventh grade. She was just drunk and... I just thought she was hot and so...things happened, and we did it."

"Hell yeah! That's what I'm talking about!" screamed Dylan as he pumped up a fist in the air.

Zander never thought he would have to lie about something that serious. He felt sick about it. It was the only thing he could feel guilty about. Over anything else, he felt nothing nor cared. And now that he had lied, it kept him from getting laid just like the rest of the team.

During the evening, Zander sat in his room as he watched T.V. Samantha had come over and spoke with him. Luckily, he had no issues with her, yet. She was only there to speak with him over a few things that she had on her mind. And some other things that she was ready to be more truthful about.

"I'm glad that you allowed this. You know, considering that you're now a P3 member," she said while awkwardly staring around the room and hoping she wouldn't screw things up.

"Well, you're not somebody I hate," he replied.

"Must be a precious little life," she said.

Perfection Is Key

"It is. It takes quite some steps, but I earned it."

"Earning something means actual risks. You do know that, right?"

"Of course, I do. It's something my parents have always.... taught me."

His mind was suddenly flooded with memories of times he spent with his family making the happiest memories he could to keep his family together. He paused until he came back to reality.

"Uhm, so what did you need? Want to talk about something?"

"Uh yeah, I hope the subject 'you' doesn't bother you." She laughed nervously.

"Me?" he asked while melting into her eyes. The one thing that Zander noticed was that every time he spent a moment with Samantha, it was like everything dropped. And the real Zander came out to play.

"Yeah. I just wanted to say that in my opinion personally, I think your behavior has become a bit too much. And I kind of think you should apologize to your parents and Ryan. But again, I don't mean to make this a bother."

"Nah it's okay. I understand that yeah, maybe what I've been doing and how I've been acting has been a real pain, but I'm just going with the flow. I'm telling you, being a part of P3 is like walking down a Hollywood red carpet, and the fans are everywhere, wanting you. The flashing of cameras are stuck on you because...well, you're a king."

"Ugh! Zander, don't you remember what we discussed and what we planned to do with the school? We were going to shut it all down and ban its people and make a change. I mean, you and Ryan had technically started the whole idea."

"It's not so bad once you get to fully understand its ways. Turns out, we all need this. This luxury. This life."

Christopher Martinez

"Zander...you can't keep this up. Let's just finally expose them at Homecoming. This school has never been on the news and that is why most people hide out here and destroy. Because no one can get caught on camera."

"No Sam. If you try to pull any crap like that, then I won't have my cool anymore. P3 will destroy anyone who gets in the way."

Samantha was so disappointed. He sighed and rubbed his hand over his mouth. He continued.

"Look, you can't force or do anything to the school! There's a guard at every corner of the building and city, so once they grab a hold of what you're doing, then you'll end up in jail for who knows how long, so go ahead and try, but you won't..." Samantha dozed off.

The room was silent. It was a good moment for her. Her thoughts were running, but she knew that it would affect something. Within a second, she slowly walked towards him and kissed him.

A long-lasting kiss. One that Zander seemed to be shocked about yet enjoyed.

"What the hell was that?" he asked.

"If you can't do it for anyone as for your parents or Ryan, then do it for your girlfriend."

"G-girlfriend? So, now we're dating? Sam, this is crazy. What's happening?" There was no denying it. He knew he was in love.

"I swear from my heart that the moment you walked into this city, I had my eyes glued to your eyes! I've been there from the start, and I've made you feel accepted. For whom you are! Not what they think you should be. P3 is a game. One that once you roll the dice, you can't win, and it stays on loop. Zander, your parents are what made you the kindhearted, blissful, charming young man. And Ryan made nothing of you. Ryan is a football star, and he was more built than you were, yet he never changed you or showed you up. You've just become a young man who has no future now. So, until you see Zander, the *true* Zander....give me a call. We'll all be waiting."

Zander sat in silence and Samantha became emotional. But she left without a doubt.

He thought deeply over what she had said, and it was hitting back hard. Like karma. But just before he could open the door to apologize, his phone rang. Dylan tried contacting him. He ignored it and laid down in silence with all the thoughts of pressure on his mind. It's like his entire body had become numb.

As it had become evening. Zander spent all day with Liam, trying out different styles. Outfits after outfits. One outfit he wore was a silver suit made of silk. It was shiny and sparkled in the light. He wore shades designed with silver and gold along with a little white.

Along the edges of the coat was a pattern design of glitter. His shoes were perfectly curved and black as a woman's nails. He wore three shiny rings covered in tiny diamonds and chains along the neck and wrists. His hair was full of gel and had a hat to top it all off.

"Man! This is going to be such a fashionable night! You're going to rock that stage bro!" Liam said. Zander slightly smiled.

"You sure it's not too much? I mean it's just high school, we don't need to have a costume change."

"Sure. But you might want to think about it. If you don't make my style happy, then what good are you for?" Zander remained silent. Liam's smirk was a very teasing glare. One that sometimes had Zander feeling a little uneasy. Like if Liam had this superpower to make the room spin and your feet felt light on air.

They continued until about an hour later. A knock came to his door. He had Zander standing with his arms stretched out and a measuring tape around his waist.

Christopher Martinez

"Come in!" Liam hollered. The door swung open as a young woman came rushing in with a small box in her hands.

"Hey babe! Guess what I got you." She handed over the small box as Liam opened it and found an expensive-looking watch. His eyes almost dropped out with how glorious it looked.

"Wow baby, this must've cost you millions!"

"Awe it's cute how you act like that such a large amount of money," she said as Zander made an expression.

She turned her attention towards Zander standing in his fancy suit. Throughout the whole moment, Zander couldn't help but wonder, *how are these guys landing the hottest girls in the city?*

I guess it was because of their charm, but it seemed a lot more than that. The girl began to throw a little bit of her hair back as she walked towards him.

"And who's your friend here?" Liam stitched the silky jacket together as he spoke without even sharing a look.

"The newest member of P3. I'm getting him to test some more of my work."

"Mm, well you sure are a perf, aren't you?" she asked as she seductively twirled her hair around her finger and sucked on her sucker. Zander gave a faint smile. This one too? God, the guy was tortured enough, wasn't he?

"Alright, so what do you think of this shade with this light blue tie?" asked Liam as he held them up to Zander's face.

"Seems pretty tight to me," he said while slightly shrugging his shoulders and letting out a small laugh. Liam then dropped some things and put his arm around his girlfriend.

"Oh, and this is my girl, Josie Jones. She's been my little peach for three years and I can't imagine my life without her." She gave a seductive smile and rested her head on his shoulder.

Perfection Is Key

"Ah shit, I forgot my pins. I'll be right back," said Liam as he ran out the room. Zander knew what was going to happen as he stepped down and tried to head out as well. Josie stopped him with her hand gliding across his chest.

"Wait, sorry if I sound desperate or something, but what do you say we go and get some drinks later on today?" He slowly moved her hand away. He then walked over to the mini desk full of layered clothing. He took off the sparkly jacket and placed it onto the table.

"Uhm, I'm not sure your boyfriend would be too happy with that."

"Ugh, he's going with us. Obviously. Look, I'm just saying it would be great to do so that we can get to know each other a bit more." She seemed too good to be true. Liam walked back in as he gave Zander a glare. He began to put the small box of pins onto the table.

"Whoa, what are you doing? I wasn't entirely done you know."

"Sorry, your girl was just asking if we can all go get some drinks later. You cool with that?" Liam crossed his arms as he scoffed.

"Of course. Could use a time out from all this. But you, my good sir, are not going dressed like that. Maybe I can let you borrow one of my tuxes." He rushed off towards the closet.

Zander's parents were preparing for a dinner date. They each stood in the living room. Melissa wore a beautiful, slim dress. She almost looked like an opera singer. Simon wore his regular tuxedo as he then twisted his watch in a weird way.

"Oh, that's cool. I didn't know your watch could do that," said Zander while grabbing his father's wrist. His parents were still angry with him, but they still loved him. Simon swung his arm away from Zander.

Christopher Martinez

"It's not a toy," his brows up, revealing an expression that Zander hadn't seen since he was nine, getting in trouble.

"Dinner's in the fridge. We'll be home probably late, so in case you want a snack later, then help yourself," said Melissa as she switched her purse from one hand to the other.

"Alright. But where are you guys off to now?" asked Zander in an annoyed tone.

"That's personal. Once again, none of your business. I thought we talked about this," said Simon with a serious tone.

Zander glanced over at his mother who seemed to try and avoid all eye contact.

The two finally walked out. Zander felt suspicious about the two. This left him in a scheming mood. He began searching through his parents' bedroom to find any money they had stashed away. Why? For Homecoming night. He planned on buying condoms. The more he searched, the more he couldn't find anything. He finally went through some drawers.

One pull of a drawer and Zander noticed some material that seemed strange. In his mother's drawer, he found a pair of earrings. He carried them out when he suddenly dropped one. A sudden laser shot out and zapped a portrait of Mona Lisa hanging above the vanity set.

In his father's, he found a pair of sunglasses that looked normal. A sudden squeeze of a side button, and a blue light turned on right at the top right corner of the lens. He slowly put them on, and he was exposed to a hologram of a map to the city. He was in a state of shock, he couldn't even think.

"Who looks immature now?" he asked while smirking at the map. This was Zander's chance to finally bring some chaos to the family.

Chapter Seven
Spill It!

Simon and Melissa Robbins were no ordinary parents. They could make the world think they were a struggling family with a low budget and a normal teenager in the house. But here's the part of the story where every little secret came rolling down the hill. Nothing stays secret forever.

After a couple of hours, Mr. & Mrs. Robbins had come home from their dinner date. Zander was sitting on the couch with the mini gadgets in his hands.

"Zander...why are you still awake? It's late now and you have school tomorrow," said Simon as he looked like a bus just ran over him.

"And I assume you have a murder to commit?" he responded.

"Excuse me?"

Zander came to his feet while dropping the items onto the coffee table. His head held up high and a face that looked like he had just won the world's largest heavy medal.

"Yeah. You heard me." They each looked at each other with a blank face. The tension in the room was rising, and Melissa felt her anger rise.

"What are you doing with my jewelry?!" screamed Melissa as she threw her coat onto the arm of the couch. "Why were you in our room? We've specifically demanded you to never be in there without permission. Much less without us!"

Zander rolled his eyes at her.

Christopher Martinez

"Yeah, and I now know why! You two are holding some weird ass weapons in this house. What the hell are we, some sort of serial killers involved with some cult?!"

Melissa stared at her husband. He nodded and shrugged.

"Okay. I guess it's time to announce the secret."

They each sat down, and Melissa grew nervous. Simon still believed that Zander wasn't ready to hear the news yet, but he figured that telling the truth would probably be the best. The tea was spilled, might as well clean it.

"So, your father and I have kept this from you for your entire life... but now you must know. And I just want you to understand that we never meant for it to come to you this way. And we didn't hide it to be selfish," she said. She placed her hand on Zander's knee. He sat still. Anxious to hear what the secret was.

"We never wanted to hide it at all. But it seemed best," continued Simon.

"We are secret agents. Spies. And the only reason we moved here was because of a huge mission. There's an evil-plotting person who plans on burning all the school and its students on Homecoming night. We still haven't figured out his identity yet, but we will soon. All the paperwork, all the late nights, it's just us doing research or battling their henchmen."

"And you couldn't have warned me earlier!?" Zander said.

"Well honey, why should we have? We know we're going to stop him. Whoever it might be. But look, I think it was great, because you weren't involved. I didn't have to worry about somebody hurting my baby."

Zander was too stunned to even speak. He shook his head and processed everything. He exhaled deeply. He then came to his feet.

"You guys are freaking insane! Sometimes I wonder why I even bother!" He stormed out of the room and headed upstairs.

Perfection Is Key

Later that afternoon, Zander spoke with Samantha over the phone for a good while. But soon, she had to end the conversation by doing some work at her father's business place. The more they spoke, the more she became this person who had 'so many things to do' and would end conversations with everyone as quickly as possible. Zander started questioning her moves. But overall, he tried to ignore it and not worry.

Homecoming drew nearer, and one school day, after lunch, Zander had been called to the principal's office. He approached the door and knocked lightly.

"Principal Shue? It's me, Zander. You wanted to see me?" The door was cracked open, and I guess Mr. Shue couldn't hear him. Zander peeked through and found him talking with Dylan.

"Look, all I know is that I can't wait to get the hell up out of here! Once the school year's over, we'll have all the money. And I'm going to take it far away from here! Everyone can suffer a pain just like I had to!" Mr. Shue said.

"I mean, there's a lot of people out there who can still be more powerful than you, so you still might have some competition. I think we should try and at least get some people to go with us," said Dylan.

"No. I make the rules and I'll break some others if needed."

"Dad, just calm down. This isn't a thriller show–"

"Shh! You can't call me Dad! The day we burn this place down, then we can try to be some sort of family."

Zander couldn't believe what he heard. Finding out Dylan was Principal Shue's son made everything feel a little scary. But by realizing how the two share a good personality and have the same smile, why didn't he notice before? Zander suddenly remembered Alyssa's words.

Christopher Martinez

"He gave him up to foster care, he just wasn't ready. No one's ever gotten clues or ideas as to who it could be."

The door swung open. There stood Dylan. His obnoxious smirk ran across his face. Zander slightly stepped back, only to realize he shouldn't go any further. He didn't want to look guilty of anything. Standing near Dylan felt like standing next to your worst enemy who could strike at any minute.

"Hey there Z, what are you doing up here? You get in trouble?" he asked.

"Uh, I don't think so, I don't know why I'm up here." His palms began to sweat. He tried hiding the fact that he was wiping them off onto his pants. Dylan pulled out a toothpick and placed it in his mouth. He raised an eyebrow.

"Oh, Principal Shue told me that you did some skipping the other day. Sounded like fun. Wish I was there."

"I only did that cause Liam wanted to test some outfits out on me." Mr. Shue's face popped out of nowhere. He stood by and the boys stared back at him. He creased his eyebrows. Dylan began to walk away while giving a quick wink at Zander.

"Alright, I'm headed out. Good luck in there man."

As Zander stepped into the office, he sat down. Though his stomach felt like a twisted pretzel. He's never feared Mr. Shue before. His mind went blank, and now he sat back in the chair without a care in the world.

"So, what am I here for?"

"Kid, you're here for the three classes that you skipped yesterday!! You think Rampage is just an option?"

"No. Well, kind of. Dylan said I don't really have to be here all the time," he said as he laughed a bit and rubbed his forehead.

"Dylan is a pathetic beast! He wants attention and praise! Look he and I have some things to do, so let's just-"

Perfection Is Key

"I know, I know...because you guys have a big plan to get loaded and burn this place to the ground. You guys are basically the ones who want to burn down the school and try to get away with it." Mr. Shue shot him a confused look. But at the same time, you could tell his anger was starting to build up.

"How the hell do you know that?"

"You got a big mouth buddy." Zander leaned forward as he glared at Principal Shue's eyes, but Shue struck back.

"Look! Detention for three Saturdays and if they are not done, you'll be stuck in after school doing military practice for a month!"

"Military Practice? What is that?"

"The only place that will bust your ass and make you witness what true hell is! Sound exciting? I sure hope so."

Zander rolled his eyes and sighed as he grabbed his stuff and left. Shue sat down speechless. Fixing his tie, he stared at the door and wondered to himself if Zander even knew about Dylan being his son.

Meanwhile, James had come downstairs to talk with his parents about wanting more equipment for his workout routine. His sweaty face practically dripped on the floor.

"Dad, I really need more workout weights. I'm starting to look loose and bony. You know, I had to do at least ten more reps per workout, and I still barely got a few more pounds in. You know I can't look unbalanced. You happen to have any extras?"

"You look as perfect as you have always been, James!" Mr. Coleman said as he let out a small laugh. He turned his attention back to reading his newspaper.

"No, I'm not! I'll end up looking like a skinny little boy who will be thrown into dirt. You know that one kid who was out of school for

Christopher Martinez

two weeks? It was because he wasn't eating, and it made him look like a damn skeleton. I could never be in the same position as him."

"Alright son, calm down. There's some old equipment that your uncle left behind before he moved out. I believe they're in the basement. C'mon, let's go look."

As they each headed down to the basement, they searched through old boxes full of old belongings, old toys, and broken objects. They searched for a while and couldn't really find much of anything. James had ended up finding a box titled 'Family,' and grabbed it.

"Hm. Old family photos huh? I barely remember what I was like as a kid. I guess because I always focused on making my body perfect." His father's reaction became blank.

"Uhm son, I would just leave that alone. Your mother doesn't like me or anyone to go through those. Let's just keep looking for the weights yeah?" James ignored him and kept looking at all the memories. Pictures of carnival trips, going out to eat, to the movies, shopping, birthdays, graduation of his parents, and many other events. He suddenly grabbed one of the family portraits. He smiled.

"I was such a baby in this photo," he said.

"Yeah..." Mr. Coleman's voice began to trail off. "I think I saw some punching bags in the back over here, so if you want to..." Mr. Coleman suddenly caught James staring deep at the photo. He closed his eyes and sighed as his face fell.

James had noticed the portrait being folded on one side. Questioning the random fold, James turned it over and found himself holding a baby girl under his right arm.

"Whoa. Who's this?"

"That was one of your cousins. Your aunt and uncle wanted us to take another picture with her and so..." James turned it over to see writing on the back.

Perfection Is Key

Couple: Jamie & Lisa Coleman
Kids: James & Amber Coleman.

James widened his eyes. His father put a hand on his shoulder, but James shoved it away. He gave a pause as he stared carefully at the picture.

"James," Mr. Coleman began.

"I have a sister?!" he screamed. His anger rose.

"You used to. But there's a rea-"

"Where is she?"

His father knew that this family secret was no longer safe. He didn't want to keep it from him, but it for the best in the time.

"...she's in a different state. With a different family." James became confused and had no words for the news of having a long-lost sister. There was nothing else to feel or even say now. He rushed past his father and headed back upstairs. He stood in the kitchen where his mother was washing dishes.

"Why didn't you tell me I had a long-lost sister!? Or better yet, why didn't you keep her?!"

Mrs. Coleman's eyes widened, and she noticed the photo sitting by the tip of his fingers. His veins popped out of his hands with all the tight gripping.

"Oh sweetie... how'd you find that?" she asked. Her tone was serious and disappointed.

"What in the hell is going on here?" he asked. His eyes began to burn as he tried holding back the tears that were flooding his eyes. His mother remained speechless, he dropped the picture and ran upstairs in anger.

His father then walked out of the basement. He slowly shrugged his shoulders at her as she began to tear up. He kissed her forehead.

Christopher Martinez

"Hey, it's alright. We've talked about this. It was bound to happen. He was going to find out anyways. I'll go talk to him." He kissed her forehead one more time before heading upstairs.

Liam and Zander were testing more outfits. Different sizes, different colored accessories, and trying to choose between having regular, fancy looking shoes, or boots. Zander had become more of a dress-up doll for Liam. Not everyone is a model, but Liam was all about style. You had to have it. Or even he would ruin you.

"Bro, this suit is sucking the air out of me. Are we done with this one yet? Maybe it's just the leather," said Zander as he tried moving his arms in the tight coat.

"You're fine." Liam replied. "Oh. It's like looking at a masterpiece. I mean, it was made by me, so technically, it is."

"I'm actually glad I finally look like the god of glam."

"You're welcome. But remember, I'm the god of glam." Zander chuckled as his phone rang. It was Samantha calling. He answered.

"Hey...yeah...oh okay. Well maybe after the movies, we can head out and get..." His voice trailed off and the silence of the room was awkward. Liam continued measuring the clothes and stitching as he listened. Zander's face fell. "Um okay. But call me when you get done," he continued. He ended the call and placed his phone back onto the table.

"What was that about?" asked Liam.

"I don't even know man. Every time we talk, she ends up cutting off and just leaves. Should I be worried?"

"Dude, girls have their weird ways. For all you know, she's probably trying to get you in her pants. Who is she anyways?"

"Samantha. Samantha Shaw." Liam paused to think until he shrugged his shoulders.

"Don't know her. Doesn't really sound familiar. Then again, none of the people I've helped do." He laughed.

"She's not just any girl. I feel like I could go my whole life with her. She's a pretty special one, you know?"

"Mm, good luck with that. So, you two are going to be hooking up tonight after Homecoming?" asked Liam as he danced his eyebrows up and down.

"Oh yeah man. We've planned everything," he lied.

"Ahhhh look at you!" Liam's phone buzzed. He pulled it out from his pocket when suddenly his face became a frown. He shoved it onto the table and continued sewing. The phone buzzed three more times. Zander swapped it up in his hands.

"Who's texting you? You got your hoes all up on you or what?"

"Hey! What's the matter with you? Give it back!" The two fought for a moment.

Zander suddenly stared at three messages. They were hateful, ugly, nasty comments. Liam snatched it back and continued sewing.

"Liam...who was that? Why were they saying all those horrible things to you?"

"It's nothing. And next time you touch my phone, I'll get your ass pinned." His face seemed annoyed.

"Is someone bullying you?" Liam stopped and let out a deep sigh. He closed the bedroom door and lowered his voice. Another heavy sigh ran out of his mouth.

"Okay. If I tell you something so secretive, do you swear on your life to never tell anyone? Not even the guys."

"Of course." Liam was hesitant.

"Yes. I'm...I've been getting bullied. There's this guy in my chemistry class and for some reason, he's never liked me. He's hated me since childhood. I tried reporting him, my parents tried, but he was so good at playing the victim. All those old issues got my family and I

Christopher Martinez

banned from the city for three days one time. That's how I became a part of P3. Dylan helped me out of the situation and got the guy to stop. Made his life a living hell. And he threatened him with death and the dude promised to leave me alone. But Dylan never knew that after only a couple of years went by, the dickhead kept at it."

"Why didn't you tell anyone?" asked Zander. Even though he knew he shouldn't have continued the conversation. It could have been a very hard thing for Liam to discuss.

"It's too much to deal with. Besides, here I can at least live the life that keeps me happy. He can only type mean things to me. There's no physical harm."

"Well, you can't just NOT do anything. I would tell Principal Shue or something. Couldn't they scare him away?"

"Shue wouldn't care. He's more into Dylan than he ever is with James and I."

"Okay, well you got to tell someone. Why don't we-"

"No!" He let out a deep sigh as he flopped down onto the nearby chair. "Just forget it. Alright? The dude's a prick. He'll never learn his lesson, and if I'm a ruler here at Rampage, scaring off other people, everything will be okay."

It may have been Liam's decision, but Zander couldn't help but feel sorry for him. How can you be king at one place, yet a victim at another?

After a while, Zander lay in his bed and stared up at the ceiling. He could only think about Liam and his crazy spy parents. The thoughts were overwhelming. He looked over at his drawer and saw all the alcohol he had over the past few weeks. He grabbed a brand new bottle and began drinking from the scratch.

Perfection Is Key

A few minutes later, Zander was still up and drunk. Not too drunk. But enough to make him feel loose and sort of free from everything. His doorbell rang, interrupting his relaxing time. He answered to find Samantha as she smiled. Her backpack in her hands.

"Hey, I know it's late, but I had to talk to you about something. Can I come in?" Zander looked confused at first as he gestured for her to walk in. She sat nervously. Her eyes searched the room like there were security cameras watching 24/7.

"What's up?" asked Zander as he sat next to her. His eyes were dead. He smelled completely like alcohol, but that wasn't stopping anything.

"Now that we're dating, we shouldn't keep secrets, right?"

"Of course. And we can be open and trusted. For me, personally for me, I just want us to grow. Hope that isn't too soon." She giggled at his words as she looked down.

"No, that's never too soon. But..." She sighed a bit as he watched her with a worried look.

"What's wrong?" She felt sick to her stomach.

"Look, I have something to confess and... I don't know how you'll take it."

"Please, having secrets is one of my best qualities. Unless you've got a prison record and you're about to murder me." She laughed.

"Promise you won't tell anyone? Not that it's much of a secret," she said while rolling her eyes a bit. Her breath sounded exhausted.

"Who am I going to tell? I go to one quinceanera a year," he said with a blank face.

"I don't expect you to continue being my boyfriend after this, but I hope you still speak with me." He shrugged his shoulders.

Christopher Martinez

"Hit me with your best shot." She let out a heavy sigh and grabbed her backpack. She slowly pulled out a long, luscious red wig. Curly with black streaks. It was stunning.

"I'm your new friend...Alyssa Reed."

Zander was at a complete loss for words. He sat still. He wasn't entirely sure how to react.

"That...is...AMAZING!" He leaped up from his seat.

"W-what? You're okay with this?"

"What, how could I not be okay with this? This shows that both of us are suffering! We could seriously change things up here if we start now!"

"Uhm, didn't you forget about who you are? You're an official member of P3," she said.

"Well, remember, Ryan..." Zander began to think about his best friend. He realized that there was going to be no change if he wasn't going to follow through with a plan. He knew deep down that he wasn't acting like himself anymore. P3 had a dark power over him.

"Look, again, this is not something we should get involved in. I think if we talk with someone, then maybe they can help us make a change, but otherwise, it's far too dangerous. I thought we spoke about this. You don't know P3 like I do. They will do everything they can in their little power to try and destroy you! To them, we're nothing. It's only a matter of time that they shoot you down too."

"I know I've been a pain in the ass, but I can handle it. Ryan may not be on good terms with me, but that doesn't mean I wasn't going to stick to the plan. I mean, c'mon Sam! I know we can still face this challenge! We'll probably just start over with-"

"No, you're missing the point! Those three are the worst people around here and we had a whole plan to take them down. But again, you're not yourself anymore. You're like an exact twin of Dylan.

Perfection Is Key

You have to trust me; this popularity isn't going to get you success. It won't bring you more friends or even family."

Zander's face fell. He pulled her into his arms.

"Okay. Okay, I'm sorry. Look, I want to make things right, but-"

"But you're so caught up in the popular world, it's not coming any sooner. We're still stuck in the same rounds." He glanced at her as he then gave a small smile.

Just when he thought he had heard enough, the night wasn't quite over. The war was just beginning. Zander received a message from Miranda. She asked to speak with him. Zander hardly knew the girl, but he was too kind. He loved being friendly to everyone he ever met.

The two sat at the round table that stood centered in the Coffee Shop. To make things more awkward, Kristal and Mae had to tag along.

"I know that we don't entirely know each other, but that is why I brought you here. We've all agreed to have a night out and just get to know each other better. What do you think?"

"James says you guys should be known," said Kristal as they each giggled. Josie tossed a strand of her hair over her shoulder.

"I hope you can be comfortable with this. I mean we just figured it would be helpful, and plus we can be great friends," said Josie while placing her hand on top of Zander's.

"And are the guys okay with this?" he asked with a shaky voice. Nothing else could possibly make him feel more unsteady.

"You're an official member, aren't you?" asked Miranda with a slight eyebrow lift. Zander nodded with a smirk. The reminder that you're practically worshipped brought joy to Zander sometimes.

Christopher Martinez

"Alright then. We will meet at the P3 Adulthood and probably get some meals or something. Sound good?" She smiled at him, her lashes sparkling in the distant light.

"Wait, P3 has their own Bar?!" His eyes grew wide. Josie laughed.

"Not a bar, but a strip club. Which we work at." They each lifted their eyes as they took pride in what they did.

Zander's shoulders tensed up as he gave a slight smile. After all the tiny flirty moments he experienced with these girls, Zander couldn't find his trust in them. But his mind told him to ignore all the little dramas and take a ride on the strip club train. It's what guys do when their head is all tied up with fame and wealth. Or even women. Zander had now landed in a trap. There was no turning back.

Chapter Eight
Three Black Queens

Another regular Monday, and Miranda, Kristal, and Josie were ready to steam up some things around town. They each walked in the girl's bathroom as they hogged a whole mirror to themselves. While applying more makeup or more lipstick, they each discussed their plan to rid Zander of P3 for good.

"OMG, can you believe James wants to have a baby? I honestly don't think that is something we need to help with our relationship. Ugh, he gets on my nerves sometimes. I mean, I don't want to be like my own damn mother who gets knocked up every week," said Kristal.

"Oh, come on, I think you would make a great mother! Can you just imagine a little Kristal running around? Awe, I would love to see that," said Josie. Kristal gave a smile as she sort of blushed. She stroked her hair and admired her reflection.

"Well, I feel like it would be awesome if I could start a family with such a hottie like James, but I don't know, I don't feel like we're ready," said Josie.

"Ugh, would you two shut up already? Look, we need to go to the mall after school today for our plan to work. We really need to make sure that we look sexy enough for Zander to be tricked," said Miranda.

"Mm, I know, I've got us all covered already. Since the guys are clueless, Liam is going to buy us dresses that only he can get. Isn't he awesome?" The girls smiled as they felt devious. Miranda applied more lipstick and ran her hands through her hair. It was medium length as the curls rolled in a perfect shape over her shoulders.

Christopher Martinez

"Alright, let's get out of here. I'm starting to feel steamy. And I need to find Dylan before Lunch, he's going to buy me something so that I don't have to starve." She smiled while flipping her hair. They each strutted out. Little did they realize someone else was in the room.

She slowly opened the stall door, and she held her phone close to her chest. She remained silent and tried to process what had happened.

"Those bitches. P3 is enough damage for Zander," said Samantha as she stepped out of the stall. Her luscious red wig drooping down over her shoulders. She could barely breathe in the tight sparkling skirts that she wore. As a girlfriend, she knew exactly what she had to do. What other girl would be willing to protect Zander?

"Zander, we need to talk." Samantha slid down to her seat as she slightly dragged her tray towards her chest. Zander chewed on the little steak that lay on his tray. Along with a bottle of juice and a small bottle of water.

"I told Coach Ross that it was one time! I didn't mean to drink that much water," he protested as Samantha gave a disgusted look.

"Ewe. No, I just overheard Miranda and her little posse talking in the girl's room, and they aren't just planning to have a night out with you. They have more than that going up their sleeves."

"What do you mean? Those girls are nice. I was even lucky enough to take them out. That's not something you can get every day."

"Well, turns out they're not all that sweet. They obviously want to turn the guys against you! They're going to make a fool out of you! They were talking about tricking you in their plan tonight. It's bad enough that you're under Dylan's wing, but now that you're getting involved with the girls, things are only going to get worse. Your kingdom has come to an end."

"Sa-... I mean, Alyssa, look I would've known if they had something against me. After your speech about me becoming a horrible person, I don't need any more lectures."

"Zander... This isn't a game anymore. Okay, they're going to destroy you! Promise me you won't go." His face remained blank as he continued to chew up his food.

"I can take care of myself." Samantha rolled her eyes as she began to feel frustrated with him. Her voice cracked as she spoke.

"Come on! You know that I'm right. You really need to start thinking about this. Trust me, I won't stop until you come to your senses! You want to help me make a change, right? Then listen to me!"

He leaned over her shoulder.

"Sam, I need you to be my girlfriend, not my boss." His tone felt harsh as his face fell flat.

"Fine. Don't come crying to me when you wake up in the hospital bed," she said while leaning back in her chair, picking at her food.

The two ignored each other for the rest of the day.

As soon as Zander stepped into his house, his phone rang as he answered. Sometimes talking with Dylan was nerve-racking. Almost like getting ready to speak with a mafia boss.

"Hey man, what's up?"

"Hey, the girls are at the club. Remember what I said, protect them at all costs. If something happens, you won't even get to see the light of a new day! And make sure you have them back by nine."

Even though he felt his heart jump up into his throat, Zander smirked with an expression that made him look like he knew

Christopher Martinez

everything about girls and what impressed them. He lifted his brow and his shiny teeth sparkled in the light.

Zander and the girls sat around the bar and the DJ played loud music on the huge stage. Pink and red lights lay across the edges of the roof, as the room was full of booths. Strippers danced their best within each room. The girls leaned against the wall as their bodies were exposed to the whole audience. Their bikinis sat tightly against their skin. Miranda twirled her hair as she stared around the room.

"You know, do you guys ever feel uncomfortable doing this job? I mean, you all have a boyfriend who would do anything to make sure you're pleased, but then you come here to do this...I would feel like a cheater. But that's just my opinion," said Zander.

"James likes to show me off, so he really doesn't care that I do this job. And I really doubt the other guys are bothered as well. People could call us all kinds of names and it wouldn't bother us because this is just our job," said Kristal with a shrug.

"Sometimes Dylan and I have our own little stripping sessions at home. It can get kinky sometimes too. He's obsessed with being kinky," continued Miranda. Josie gave a tense stare at all the guys that walked past her.

"What about you Josie? Do you and Liam do anything?" asked Zander. She smiled like she was a little girl who had just won a huge teddy bear. She moved a strand of her hair out of her eye and tucked it behind her ear.

"Well let's just say we take things smoothly," she said.

Zander lifted his brows as he seemed impressed. Miranda then offered a drink. She gazed into his eyes.

"Want a drink? I bet it'll make you feel better. After all of today's work. You boys sure do a lot of work. I bet it gets tiring having to boss people around." She rubbed his arm. The muscle printing through his shirt. He grabbed the drink as Kristal and Josie took one from the small bar behind them. Kristal began to play around with the few buttons on Zander's collared shirt.

"You know you can take this off in case you happen to get too hot or something," said Kristal. Her eyes twinkled in the pink light.

"Uh thanks. I think I would know that by now." He smiled awkwardly while taking another sip from his drink. Josie suddenly grabbed his arm and pulled him to a nearby room.

"C'mon, you have to come watch us do a new dance that we made up for the boys! We want to know what you think," she said while rushing behind a tall set of dark curtains.

Zander sat down in the center of the huge, curved couch. The walls were covered in posters of the boys either modeling by themselves or with the girls. Material and decor sat around the area as if it were some beautiful hotel suite inside an expensive house. He stretched out his arms across the seat and relaxed. Miranda and the girls hopped up onto the luxurious table that held a gold pole in the middle of it. The songs that played in the background made the moment intense.

Within seconds, the girls started doing a routine and caressed Zander in the best way possible. Zander began to feel light-headed. He rubbed his head as he squinted around the room. His vision started to shake. He kept cheering the girls on like the effects were nothing to him.

Before he could focus on what exactly was happening to him, Miranda stepped down and she began to unhook her bra, exposing her breasts. She leaned in on Zander. He admired her body. The two then started kissing and Kristal and Josie also stepped down to join in. They stripped him from his shirt as they unbuckled his pants. Zander smiled as he laid his head back with a pleasing feeling. It was a deep desire

Christopher Martinez

he's always wanted to experience, but he knew it would bring some danger.

"Give me a kiss baby," he said while grabbing Miranda's head. Kristal groped him as Josie slid her hand across his muscular arm. They all giggled in unison. He knew in the back of his head that it was all wrong, but there was no control.

Miranda's eyebrows danced up as she smirked at Kristal and Josie. She flipped herself under Zander as she seductively slid her leg across his leg.

This was the moment when Zander's perfect world shook. It was like an earthquake struck, and his kingdom came tumbling down. Miranda texted Dylan a few minutes earlier to go ahead and meet up with her at the club. Only to have Zander caught up in a strong web.

Miranda: Babe, come get us, Zander has been acting strange ever since he got here and I'm afraid he's going to try and do something to us. Please hurry!

After about an hour, the guys showed up to the club. Though they sure weren't happy. They stormed through the doors. Dylan took complete action. The two buff men guarding the curtain slid them open. Zander was topless with unbuckled pants, a sweaty body, and messy hair. He was hovering over the girls. They each sat with worried faces. As if Zander had more of an intention to rape them. He almost looked like he was high.

Dylan became furious as he pulled Zander away from the girls. Zander laughed as if what he was just doing wasn't wrong. But who could blame him when he's been numbed.

"The hell do you think you're doing man!! Is this funny to you!? This is the kind of shit you pull?!" Dylan pinned Zander against the wall as his face became an extreme red. Kristal and Josie ran up to James and Liam. The fake fear brushed over their faces. Miranda snapped on her bra again as she tried pulling Dylan away from Zander.

"C'mon, let's just get out of here!! Just let him walk home!! He is already banned from here! And he should be expelled from P3!!"

Dylan threw a punch at Zander's nose as he fell to the ground. He grabbed onto Miranda's arm and they were each out of sight.

Zander limped his way out to the alley as he fell to the ground. He held his stomach as the pain grew. Cars were driving and honking in the background as the alley only had one very dimmed light on the side of the building. The rain poured and cats walked along the edges of the dumpsters. He stared at both sides as he felt lost and alone. It was like being dumped in a pile of garbage.

Samantha suddenly came rushing out from behind a dark wall. Holding an umbrella as she was covered in a black raincoat and disguised as Alyssa.

"Zander, get up. C'mon." She lifted him up as he stared at her face. He couldn't recognize her. Everything was beginning to look blurry.

"S-s-Sam? What are you doing out here?"

"Waiting for your dumbass to get the hell out of there. I told you that they had something devious up their sleeve. And now P3 hates you and they're going to raise some serious hell." She dragged him to her car and the two were headed home.

Zander updated his parents on everything that had happened. No matter what secrets or bad issues there were, Simon and Melissa wouldn't stop at nothing to protect their son. They stared at Zander as if he had just been through some bad wreck. Their expressions seem

Christopher Martinez

worried. Zander laid on the couch while his eyes barely stood open. He laughed.

"So how do you know that they did this on purpose?" asked Melissa while crossing her arms. They stood near a corner.

"The girls were speaking about it in the bathroom during school the other day. I tried to warn him, but he wouldn't listen. He's so caught up in wanting to be popular! But now... Dylan hates him. Who knows what issues he could bring to his life now? You guys have no idea how far Dylan will go to make sure his enemies suffer," said Samantha. She rubbed her forehead while letting out a heavy sigh.

"Okay, then we will go and find these girls and turn things back to the way they were. I'd say we trick them into thinking there's a party, then wrapping them up in some sizzling rope!" Melissa said with a smirk. Simon gave her a glance.

"Honey, no, we wanted Zander to leave that group in the first place! Maybe now we can try and turn his mindset around. That sounds awesome, right?" Melissa nodded as Simon then pulled her toward his chest. They each stared at Zander as he seemed to finally be asleep.

"I guess we'll see what happens. The only thing we can do right now is be there for him. Both family and friend," said Samantha as she crossed her arms. They each headed off to bed as they waited eagerly for tomorrow. More importantly, for Dylan.

Chapter Nine
Vengeance on Rampage

After a week, it was officially time for Homecoming. And it was about to go from beautiful to burned. Ryan sat with an angry face, messy hair, sleepless eyes, and a huge set up of technology to trigger the spark to set the fire. He hadn't been himself since the day he and Zander argued. Everything began to roll downhill from there. Bottles lay all over the floor as his head felt like it was about to explode. He smirked deviously, he began hacking into all sorts of electric boxes among the building and began turning off the power. Little did he know, his parents were warned about Zander. Now that he was in danger, it was only good to have as much support from people as possible.

"Oh, Hi Mr. & Mrs. Robbins, how are you-" Before Mrs. Williams could finish her sentence, Melissa pulled out her small gun gadget.

"Where is your son? He is about to do something extremely stupid!"

"What? Well, he's upstairs in his room. What is he doing?" Melissa then stepped inside as she rushed up to Ryan's room.

"Please, let us handle this! We'll explain everything later," continued Simon. Their reactions suddenly turned to worry. They each ran upstairs and banged on the door. They tried opening, but it was locked to the point that only a policeman could open it.

"Ryan Williams, you open this door right now!!" demanded Simon.

"Stay out!" he replied.

Christopher Martinez

    The Robbins exchanged looks then pulled out another gun gadget as they busted out the side window and swung around the house to burst through Ryan's bedroom window. He groaned at the screen while holding a button, glaring at the two.

As for Zander, he and Sam were enjoying the party. Wine here and there, dancing, cake, and some fancy decor. Zander looked around the room. His heart pounded. All he could think about was making sure he had a way out in case Dylan tried to sneak in an attack. He tightened his hold on Samantha's hand.

    "Hey, are you okay? You've hardly touched the food or even danced," she said.

    "Uh yeah. I'm fine. I'm just wondering when...they will play a good song for us to dance to." He laughed nervously. She smiled at him.

    "Okay? I mean it's been a while now. I'm sure all the dancing songs have passed."

    "Look, I really think we should get out of here. I don't feel safe here knowing that Dylan could humiliate me in front of everyone! I know what you're going to say, but I can't help it. Being popular doesn't just mean going out and having riches and wealth, but it makes you feel powerful. Like you have the world in your hands."

    "You're talking nonsense." Before he could tell her more, Principal Shue grabbed the microphone.

    "Okay everyone! I hope you are all having a perfect night! Ahem, now, it's time to announce who will be your Homecoming Legends." Everyone cheered and hollered.

    "Your boy nominees are...Liam Dixon, James Coleman, Dylan Anderson, and Zander Robbins!"

Perfection Is Key

Zander's eyes widened at hearing his name next to Dylan's. They each stepped up onto the stage, yet Zander created a good distance between him and the boys. He stared at Dylan. It was like a lion watching for its prey to move.

"And your girl nominees are Molly Hawkins, Lisa Gamble, and Maya Blaine," continued Principal Shue.

Time ran on and while coming back to reality from his thoughts, Zander had won Homecoming Legend along with Maya Blaine. The two smiled in joy and thanked the school. Even though Zander felt the need to throw up.

It hit Midnight and Ryan was ready to push the button in his hand. There was no control over him. The blood in his eyes was front and center. It was like looking into a vampire.

"Ryan, you don't need to do this. We can all agree here that my baby boy is no longer the same, but that doesn't mean destroying everything," said Melissa. Her tone sounded sympathetic.

"I... I just want him to understand. But he left me! He abandoned all of us! He deserves to see the flames! It'll only help him realize what this all costs him." Ryan's voice cracked as his body shivered. Tears filled his eyes. The Robbins exchanged looks as they kept their small gadgets up.

"Zander can still come back, and we can do our absolute best to make him release the whole idea that popularity is the key to everything. But we would need you too," she continued as she held her hand up toward him.

"Just put the button down and disarm the whole thing," said Simon. "It's not what Zander would have wanted. He needs you more than ever. He needs you to help bring him back."

Christopher Martinez

Ryan turned slowly as he stared at Simon with an angry face, though you could tell he was fighting back the urge to break down. He then placed the button on the desk as he dropped in his spot.

Simon pushed three buttons on the keyboard as the system powered down. Ryan leaped up and screamed as he tried to reactivate everything. But before he could touch it, Melissa threw a rope that was wrapped around his chest and held him back as Simon grabbed his arm. Ryan screamed as if he just witnessed a murder. The pain poured out. It was like Ryan's mind had been freed.

"NO!" He swung his arms and legs yet gave up in seconds.

"Ryan! Listen to me, this isn't you!! We need our boy back. But we need you to help us!" Simon said. Ryan started tearing up more as he stared at Simon.

"You were wrong when you said forgiveness works Mr. Robbins. I've already forgiven him, and he still rejected our support. How can you guys not see that?" His voice shook as he choked on his words. Sweat drenched his face.

"Ryan...did you ever forgive yourself?" asked Simon.

Ryan then burst down and held onto Mr. & Mrs. Robbins as they held him back. Melissa unlocked the door and Ryan's parents walked in. They each leaped down and held onto him.

After a few minutes, Zander's parents informed him about the little drama that had just occurred with Ryan. But not only that, it was decided that they would move back home. It was their way of making sure he would be protected and removed from such a horrible place. Personally, hoping for Zander's change from the help of memories. Though this would mean leaving Samantha behind, Zander still contacted her no matter what.

Perfection Is Key

It was the last month of school, and Zander was barely making his way back to being normal. He wanted success and money. It was a hard challenge trying to put his priorities back in order.

Monroe High was not as exciting for Zander. Even though the whole school seemed to grow around his existence. But there was no more worship, no way of getting the teachers to respect you as if you were president, and there was no group to be considered a king. Ryan would try to talk to him, but there was never a response or reaction from Zander.

Everyone hated that Zander was no longer a great inspiration. His popularity was within the cool kids, who barely talked to him when he was there before.

It was a normal Wednesday and Ryan was just getting out of class as he noticed Zander by his locker. Around him were two popular jocks that he became good friends with. Ryan took a leap of faith and headed over with a smile.

"Hey buddy! I was just wondering if, uh, you'd like to go and shoot some hoops tonight with me and Alex. Just for fun, you know?"

"Mm sorry man. I've got plans. And maybe because I don't like you," he said as he and the jocks laughed. He was beginning to sound more of an ass than before.

"Aha. So, I see the rivalry continues." He gripped the strap of his backpack.

"Dude, you got to win one before giving it a title." The jocks snickered at him.

"Ugh c'mon Z. Where's my best friend at? What happened to the wise man I once knew? We were a team once. Why can't that stay?"

Christopher Martinez

"Because it's all dead. And besides, you almost killed me and my friends!" Ryan remained silent as Zander shoved his shoulder while walking away. Zander Robbins seemed to no longer exist.

Meanwhile at Rampage, Samantha became more of a hacker when it came to passwords and usernames and emails. She had gotten great access to Rampage. Her plan was to finish what she and Zander promised to each other. Destroy and expose Rampage. She snuck into the school to try and mess around with Principal Shue's computer. She chuckled a bit until a familiar voice spoke.

"Well...all I know is that I'm here for some paperwork. Your turn."

She turned to see Dylan with his arms crossed and a malice smirk across his face. Her heart started pounding like crazy for she feared what he would do. She's had so many crazy nights, she could barely move around him sometimes.

"You don't scare me. And whatever I do with my life doesn't need your big nose up in it." He pinned her up against a wall. The room was silent. It was like a hot flashback. He brushed her hair behind her ear.

"Either you tell me why you're here messing with my father's computer, or...I'm going to have to tell the whole school who you really are... Miss Samantha Shaw." She pushed his hand away.

"I have nothing to say to you. Just go home and stay there! You know you can't expose me. You don't have the authority to do that." He grabbed her arm tightly as she groaned a little in pain. She then kicked him in the crotch as he fell to the ground. "Not so fun now huh? I hope you rot."

She suddenly stormed out and ran back home. She felt safe at home, but she felt safer when Zander was around. Samantha Shaw became Alyssa Reed for a reason. To just deal with all the precious perfect life that everyone expected and have no issues until after graduation. And Dylan's known for a long time. She had plenty of stories to tell people about her experiences with Dylan. And she would have to live through hell and try to be perfect if he were to reveal her secret. But they were two weeks away from school being over. And Rampage would soon be exposed.

As for James, he could barely walk around or pay any attention to anyone. He only ever thought about the family's secret. He had been trying his best to track down his long-lost sister. Just maybe there would be some information and maybe she was in a nearby location. And in a matter of seconds, he came across a page.

'Amber Coleman. Body Still Missing Among the Lake.'

His eyes widened. He stormed downstairs and placed his laptop on the center table.
"What the hell is this?" His mother's eyes looked over at the screen.
"Where did you find this article?"
"I NEED ANSWERS AND I WANT TO KNOW WHAT THE HELL IS GOING ON!!"
"No, sweetheart, please sit and listen." James sat with a heavy sigh.
"When your sister was born, we were living back in Colorado. Everything seemed to turn out great. But....there came a time when we all headed out for a trip, and on our way home, we stopped to take pictures of this...beautiful romantic lake. And then, Amber started crying and wouldn't stop and so...I gave her some toys to play around

Christopher Martinez

with. And she wanted to play around the lake. But..." Mrs. Coleman began to cry. She could barely speak. She then continued. "She ended up falling in somehow and when I went to go find her, I swam through the whole lake and couldn't find her anywhere! So, she ended up missing. The worst thought was that she could have been dead. But the police had invested and figured she could have wandered away and got lost. So, we thought it would be best if you didn't know. We didn't want you even thinking that we had failed you as parents."

"Mom..." He grabbed her hand as he shared a sympathetic look.

"I'm so sorry James. Truly. Your father and I never wanted this to happen. And in all honesty, we were going to find the right time to tell you. Trust me when I say that."

"No, no, shh, just calm down. I'm sorry I lashed out." He stroked her head as she buried it in his chest.

"I will cherish her for my life. She would've been awesome. I know it. And this may kill me, but I will always know that I have you and dad. And I couldn't be more grateful. You guys are my world."

They each smiled as they held onto each other and cried for a moment. James hadn't felt love in a while...or in forever. He finally came to understand that there's more to life than being popular and perfect. And that's an honor.

On the other hand, Liam Dixon was still being taunted by the bully. Liam had lived in fear his whole life and took the role of being a ruler because of his past. He believed that if others intended to focus on his looks, then they would never suspect a bad thing. Their eyes would be too attached to his outfit rather than his face.

He answered an incoming call from Zander.

Perfection Is Key

"Good news! That guy who's been bullying you...he's been transferred to military school!"

"What? How? What did you do?"

"Okay, another surprise, my parents are spies and we each made a mission to expose him for who he really was! So, we questioned him, and he answered truthfully and then we fought him and got him transferred. Altogether we managed to catch him on tape. And we found this in his room. Disturbing." Liam stared at his phone as a picture popped up in his messages.

It revealed a board covered in pictures of Liam with lies and red markings and nails in almost all of them with a devil's face in the center to collect the dark energy. With a relieved head and heart, Liam felt joy. Freedom.

"Bro, this is amazing! I never thought the day would come! You have no idea what this feels like!"

"Look man, I owe you an apology. I didn't try to do all that stuff with your girl on purpose. I mean, they drugged me after all." Liam smiled as he shook his head.

"You know, all I've ever done was make others so addicted to how my style worked and not to what I could've been helped with. I went day to day with fake smiles and white lies and... I was pretty much the bully myself. I guess to make my hurt feelings go away, I passed it onto others."

"And now?" Zander knew he could make up for what he had done. Even though most of it wasn't his fault.

"...Now there are things more important to me. And that's.... that's making others feel confident in whatever they wear. Making them feel loved. It doesn't hurt to change up some ways."

"Of course. You deserve to be heard bro. And I know you can make a change. I guess we've faked it a little too long. Now it's time for the world to see what really lies beneath the surface."

Christopher Martinez

"Thanks." Liam smiled as he paused to think for a moment.

"So, am I off the hook now? Ha, you know after all the shit that happened with Josie and the girls?"

"Aha, of course man. After Alyssa told me about what happened and showed me the video she took of the girls, I had a serious talk with Josie, and we broke up."

Zander smiled. He knew he didn't want the two to split up, but it was a great thing to know that she could never hurt anyone again through the power of P3.

Zander knew what he had done was out of love. Which made him replay some honorable memories in his head. Liam learned not only true confidence, but self-worth. We're all humans. And we all can be vulnerable and free to seek help.

Chapter Ten
The Real Me

Zander Robbins was never popular. But he had a great taste in it. He was one to be cruel to whoever and get what he wanted daily. He grew more with the P3 crew. Three guys who shared their cruelty to Zander. One to improve pride, another to improve physical appearance, and one more to improve the style. Each step made Zander crush everyone around him.

One Year Later...

Zander started regaining his might. To spread love. James learned how to honor whoever made him open and wise. Liam learned to be confident in his own way. The real way. And as for P3, well...this happened.

Dylan was standing by his locker, shoving everything in his backpack. It was so elegant, it looked like a doorway to a palace. There were mirrors and glam and beauty to it. James and Liam slowly stepped up to his side. They were more nervous than relieved.

"Dylan, we have some news for you man," said James.

"Oh yeah? Like what, you both were finally winners of the 'best in bed' competition?"

"God no. Look, we're done. We're leaving P3. There's nothing left for us here. I think we've come to realize that there's more to life than all of this."

Christopher Martinez

"What?! This is a joke, huh? Guys, c'mon, just a few more days and then we'll be out of here with a world of our own! Don't you remember everything we talked about? We're going to be higher than the whole world!"

"No. All that talk on walking the world around like if it were our dog is just shabby now. You can look in that damn mirror one more time and I guarantee that it will shatter! I mean, look what we made of this city! You made this place feel like a prison. People only come here to be used. Not for anything good. And I am no longer standing for that. It honestly gets exhausting having to be this so-called 'perfect guy' who has nothing to offer. Only his body."

"Aha, you can't just walk out on me. I own you!" Dylan's face was shallow.

"Not anymore. We're done making messes for you," said Liam.

"Oh, is that so? Don't forget who helped you become a king! Without me, you're both going to be nothing. You'll just be two guys who can't get anything right and are the lamest, weakest, most embarrassing creatures who ever lived!!"

They lowered their heads. They each had thoughts running through their minds and their feelings started bouncing around like going from wall to wall.

Zander leaned against the doorway. He stared deep at Dylan's ugly smirk.

"Mm. Of course they won't forget, I mean the apple doesn't fall far from the tree, right? Or should I say weed? Seems more fitting."

"What the hell are you doing here!? Aren't you supposed to be back in that lame town of yours?"

"You mind shutting that mouth of yours for a bit? That thing moves so much boredom became my new hobby." Dylan felt rage as he then continued messing with things in his locker.

Perfection Is Key

"Look man, whatever point you're trying to reach, won't happen. I could make you my bitch too. But after what you did with my girl, you're just dead to me."

"Yeah? And I can expose your relationship with your real dad! Every game always contains at least two players. And I'm sure as hell, am not afraid of your ass."

"You don't have shit on me! You don't even know me. So yeah, Mr. Shue is my biological father, but none of y'all are going to reveal it nor is anyone going to find out." Dylan's face remained serious as his eyes looked threatening. If any of these guys were to reject that, what would happen? Dylan usually had some haunting vibes.

Zander had a recording device attached to him. Dylan calling Shue his father was all caught on it. So, Zander never showed anyone the device and he had it for the right moment. Dylan then continued packing some stuff while walking out as if nothing had happened.

"You guys alright?" asked Zander.

"Yeah bro. But thanks for the backup," said James as Zander slightly smiled.

"BUT is Principal Shue really his dad?" asked Liam as Zander gave a confused look.

"Wait, you guys never knew?"

"No. Dylan may have been our friend, but he wasn't open about a lot of things. Then again, he always felt that if we shared details about family, it would make us look weak."

"Typical. But yeah, that's his father. His biological father. I've heard their talks, and they were both planning to raise all this money they can get and leave to get all new identities and make their own government-like company that raises kids to grow up nasty and mean and vicious. Which I don't see how that's any different from here."

"The dude needs some serious help. That's all I got to say," said Liam.

Christopher Martinez

"Yeah. Well, look I got to head back. There's some things I need to help my parents with. I just came back here to catch up with Samantha. And I was walking through some areas and figured I'd stop over here to catch up with you guys. But it seemed like things were going downhill." They each headed back to the main hall.

It was finally the final day of school at Monroe. Things seemed to be normal. And just when Zander was slowly starting to enjoy a free life, the office assistant interrupted class and asked Zander to head over to the office.

He walked in and noticed Dylan sitting in one of the chairs with a devious smirk. Mr. Shue included. They suddenly headed to a private room to talk. Principal Lovington of Monroe High had smiled. Though she knew how to treat situations and she knew how to make you scared.

"Go ahead and take a seat. Let us know if you guys need anything," she said with another perky smile. She turned back around and closed the door.

"What is this, some punking shit?" asked Zander.

"Just sit down and shut your trap! We need to talk," said Principal Shue.

"About?" asked Zander.

"I hear that you threatened my son about exposing him and I? What exactly do you think you have on a pair of unstoppable men who can get exactly whatever the hell we want?" Principal Shue said.

"Sir, how about rethinking your life choices and choosing to make everyone at Rampage a better version of themselves? You think I'm going to let you get away with what you're planning? Wrong. It may take long, but I will expose you both and rid you of that place!"

Perfection Is Key

"Well... you're going to need the skill of multitasking. Miss Alyssa Reed was in school all day until after lunch, and no one's seen her ever since. Were you aware of that? So, if you want to expose us, who's going to save Alyssa? Or better yet, Samantha." Zander grew into rage.

"MAN, WHAT THE HELL HAVE YOU DONE WITH HER!? I SWEAR TO GOD I WILL END YOU!!!! I WILL CHOP YOU UP AND BURY EACH PART ALL AROUND THE CITY!!! TELL ME WHAT THE HELL YOU DID WITH HER!!!"

"Listen to yourself kid, you lost. You want pretty, luscious Sam back, then destroy that device and leave us the hell alone. Cause otherwise, you continue to blabber...and you can kiss your baby goodbye."

It felt like Zander was defeated. So many arrows stabbing through him full of regrets and fear in general. It was like being tied up in a far away place where there was no one to hear you scream and there was no way out. Zander only ever wanted to make peace. But how could he now? This battle was a challenge that he felt he could never win.

Two weeks had passed and Dylan and Shue were still in town, scheming who knows what and preparing for the runaway. Zander waited forever to finally act on his plan. To rid them of the city for good. Dylan and Shue were at a gas station near a police department. They rushed through everything as they pumped gas into the car.

Zander had his chance and was finally ready. He lowered behind a stack of wood. He then stooped over to the side of the car. Mr. Shue stood by the pump as he stared around the area. Cars passed by as the wind blew slightly. He noticed Dylan going inside. He

Christopher Martinez

suddenly placed two guns under the car as he faced them towards the store.

BANG! BANG! BANG! BANG!

The bullets flew and they shot through the building. One broke the glass window and the other ran through a car. Two policemen rushed over with their guns at everyone. Dylan and Shue put everything back into place and headed towards the car. Zander knelt in front of them as they stopped in shock. He smirked at the two as he then tossed the guns into their hands. He then backed up from behind a wall as he pointed and shouted at the two.

"IT'S THEM! THEY HAVE A GUN!" Zander screamed.

"GUNS DOWN! ON THE GROUND NOW! DO IT!" The policeman said while pointing his gun at the two. They each knelt as the other policeman cuffed their hands.

They spoke over each other as they tried blaming Zander, but the cops took them away and had them shoved into the car. Zander had done his job to finally rid the two bloodiest demons in town. He could only hope that they stayed in there for a good while.

It had been a couple of days, and Zander, Ryan, and Samantha had all spoken their view of the two with policemen and spoke about Rampage and its lifestyle. What a world of its own.

"And he had everyone under his control if they tried to leave?" asked Officer Ram.

"Yes. But not only that, they just treated everyone like crap, and they had this plan to head out and make more money by abusing the innocent minds of future generations," said Zander.

Perfection Is Key

"That's why a lot of my friends never came back to Monroe. Because Rampage had them in a whole different world. Poisoning the minds of young adults," said Ryan.

"And that's why I lied about my identity because I knew I would be hunted by their darkness...if that even makes sense," said Samantha.

They each spoke to Officer Ram for about an hour. Interviews felt like forever sometimes, and the worst part must be all the sweat from thinking you're guilty of something.

The three headed back home and felt relieved that Mr. Shue and Dylan were behind bars. Where they no longer control people.

Now unlike Junior Year, it had become a normal, drama free summer and Senior year was all in plan already by July 4th. Zander couldn't wait for what was to come next.

He knew that what he did to get rid of Dylan and Shue was kind of a wrong move, but everyone was happy that they were both gone. And a little before all of this, Samantha was found by the help of Ryan. Which wasn't too pleasant.

She stood behind his front door and rang his doorbell quite a few times.

"Thank God!! Where were you!?" said Zander as he hugged her. She gripped him as she felt so happy to see him. Her hands shook as the cold breeze slid across her back. Zander then removed his jacket to cover her. "What happened?" he continued. He rushed her inside and sat her down on the couch. She shook a bit as he tried comforting her. She rested her head on his shoulder.

"...Dylan. I wanted to tell you before, but I've been hiding away. I was just too scared."

"What do you mean? What'd he do?"

Christopher Martinez

"He's been forcing himself on me." Her body twitched like she had been in a freezer.

Zander's blood began to boil. Though, he wasn't sure how to react. The anger was like a wrecking ball wanting to burst out. He felt so guilty for not even realizing it sooner. He suddenly headed to the kitchen and took off a picture that had a safe behind it. And now that he knew about his parents being spies, he knew where their gun was hidden. Samantha stared at him as she slowly came to her feet.

"What are you doing?"

"Dylan Anderson is a piece of shit!! And he is going down for this!" He loaded the gun with a new staggered magazine.

"Zander! Now you know that isn't the right thing to do," she said as she stood tall.

"What the hell do you care for? We all hated his ass!"

"That doesn't mean he should die. That's not the right thing. You can't just call him out and then shoot him. He's not the person you want to be messing with right now. We shouldn't be wishing death upon him."

Zander slowly lowered the gun as he tried controlling his breath and anger. He nodded as he then placed the gun back into the safe.

"You're right. I'm sorry. All I can think about is putting him away in a cell. Where he and his lovely father can rot in."

Meanwhile, Zander and Ryan had a down relationship. He had so much hate towards Ryan just because he wouldn't follow along the way he saw the world. But with time, Zander had forgiven the threat Ryan had placed upon burning the school and for the argument they both had. His apologies sounded a lot more like himself. That's how Ryan knew he had his best friend back.

Perfection Is Key

Including Samantha, James, and Liam becoming part of the group, Zander felt like he was back to the real world again. With Dylan and Principal Shue being stuck in jail, Rampage was abandoned, and everyone moved to separate towns and some others moved over with Zander. Monroe was the real home. A home for everyone to be different and their true selves. With Senior Year coming along, the gang made a great pact together!

We fast forward here for a moment. Because in the entire time that every day felt like paradise, everything was normal and full of love. Summer grew closer to ending, and the gang prepared themselves for their final year.

By the end, the first day of school had arrived and everyone waited in Zander's living room. He wanted to show them an even better look for the new year. A few minutes passed and Zander yelled from behind a wall.

"Y'all ready to see the new fit?" he asked.

"Yes!" They all yelled.

He walked out in the exact same outfit he wore on his first day at Rampage. He wore his beanie, designer shirt, fancy watch, and sick vans. Simple look and it reminded everyone of his old self. He stared at them and smiled.

"Wow, you really do have it in you," said Samantha as she smiled widely.

"Now that is Zander Robbins!" said Ryan.

"Look! Skinny boy's back," said Liam teasingly.

"That's my boy," said Simon as Melissa placed her hand on his chest and smiled.

"After all this time, I never thought I would go through such a stage. Don't get me wrong, it can be super romantic in a Parisian place,

Christopher Martinez

but I already have love at home. I've got the basics to live! I've got my family, my friends, and the best part is that I have me. The real me."

"I am so proud of you," said Melissa as she hugged him.

Everyone smiled and life was back to its normal, boring feeling. Zander wanted the best for his last year. He still overthought things, he still slacked in math class, and he still acted like the crazy, stupid, yet funny and creative young man that he is.

Ugh, but the story didn't end there.

Senior year. Let's go.

Chapter Eleven
Graduation

Everyone was running and coughing as they hurried along outside. The burning building right behind them had thrown papers, and objects from all around. The flames were taking over. Distant screaming and cars honking, and the kick to the gut was hearing the sirens from all around.

"C'mon! Everyone out! Are you guys okay?" Zander stared at Samantha as she nodded, including James and Liam.

"Yeah, I hope everyone's out. I hope they're all okay," said Sam. Her coughs were sounds of someone almost vomiting.

"Where's Ryan?" asked Zander. The building collapsed as everyone screamed and ran off into their cars. Zander suddenly ran back in as the fire grew bigger around the building. Cops and firefighters were surrounding the place.

"ZANDER!" yelled Samantha in fear.

Okay...you're probably wondering what exactly is going on, or somewhat. As we already know, a building is on fire and Ryan was nowhere to be found. So, Zander ran after him. This was the part of the story where things got really interesting. How about I just take you back to the moment it all started...

It was officially Graduation Day. The gang didn't have to be at school, so they cruised around town being silly and stupid, enjoying their last

Christopher Martinez

moments before taking another huge step in their lives. Zander and Ryan laughed at their own jokes, Samantha took many photos and videos on Snapchat, James was tossing a football, and Liam was still worrying about what to wear under his gown. Zander felt so proud of himself just because he couldn't believe that he was fixing to walk the stage. They stopped by a park, and Ryan and Zander had a great way of rekindling their friendship.

"I can't believe we're finally Seniors man! It seems like yesterday we were playing tag and chasing each other around the yard," said Ryan.

"I know...I never thought we'd actually be graduating!" Zander placed his hands behind him as he leaned back and admired the sky. He turned his attention back at Ryan with a guilty face. He continued to speak. "You know, I'm sorry for what I did. I acted like a complete jerk, and I thought being popular was going to make my life become an even better one. It sure was a delicious looking apple in my eye. And I know that you know that I didn't mean any of it. And from now on, I promise I'll make sure no other person comes between our friendship. Bro, you honestly mean more than all the rest."

"Dude, I know you mean well. You just better respect me from now on! As a ruler of being the best friend anyone could have, I demand that you bow down and declare me your king," he replied in a joking manner. Zander nudged his arm as they both laughed.

The rest of the gang gestured to them to head over. They both leaped up and raced each other down there. It was a nice time to have a lot more fun before they all headed off into their adult years.

Walking the stage was all that Zander had dreamed about and it was going to be incredibly special, mainly because it was going to show his old self that life is never about how you look or what you wear.

Perfection Is Key

After a while, Samantha and Zander sat next to each other upon the swings. The wind shifted against their backs. The sound of birds chirping, and the setting was like sitting in a movie.

"You know, this year was much better with you. I couldn't have survived it without you. I don't even know what would've happened if my identity was announced to the whole place! I bet I would be depressed and crying every day and night," said Sam in a nervous tone.

"Really? And why is that?" he replied while grabbing her hand.

"I've seen you grow up and develop more in your character. I've seen what you can do to make sure nothing ends in an awfully bad situation. You honestly made me realize that I can't walk in this world acting like a Barbie forever. Eventually the mask must come off. And that no matter what happens, we can handle it." She seemed to have gazed into his eyes in a deep way. Her emotions started fluttering around.

"You know I never thought I would be dating. I always had my mind focused on my goals and just finishing high school. But then I met you. And now...life seems to have its ways." He smiled and she blushed at him.

"I really do like you. And even though things are going to get crazier by the minute, I'll always have you. Right there. By my side. And I wouldn't want to change it for anything," she said.

Zander leaned in close and the two kissed. The sunlight hit beautifully as the wind made the moment feel like they were dancing on a cloud. Zander always made sure she was healthy and pure.
He never wanted anything more than a woman like her. After the kiss, Samantha smiled.

"Well, that's the longest we've ever gone," she said.

Christopher Martinez

"And I honor that." The two then held hands as she laid her head upon his shoulder and stared at the trees. Nothing could've been better.

The day was coming closer to an end. Samantha and the boys had gone home. Ryan decided to stay a little while. And Simon and Melissa were happy to see their little boy grow into an amazing young man. They all gathered around the couch to watch some T.V.

"You know, I remember the first time you both stepped foot in the first-grade hallway. You were both excited. Even though you kept on holding onto my hand. I hated seeing you guys going to school. Only because I'm a mother. I've always wanted to keep you in my arms," said Melissa.

"And look at us now. Soon to be graduates and heading our own ways. Which I mean...doesn't mean I'll never see my best friends again. I can tell you guys that we have it in our hands now. It's one huge ball to explore, but I'll always know where to find my roots. My home," said Zander. Ryan patted his back with awe.

Melissa had grabbed a pile of old photos and brought up some great memories. Most were a bit too embarrassing, but who doesn't love some embarrassing photos. The rest of the day remained steady. The Robbins home was finally feeling like a real home.

By evening, the gang showed up at Zander's house with all their families, they had about two hours left before heading over to the auditorium. They each stood in Zander's living room. All eager for the rest of the evening.

"Okay, quick picture!" said Melissa.
"Let's do it!" replied Ryan as they all huddled up.

Perfection Is Key

"Aww. You guys look so handsome! Remember when you and Ryan were playing outside in the kiddy pool-"

"Mom..." said Zander in an embarrassing tone. Melissa gave a smile as she then raised her camera to her eye. Before she could snap a pic, Liam interrupted.

"Guys...are you seeing this?" He increased the volume of the T.V.

"Breaking news has fled the city and is having the people in a panic about the bail of Dylan Anderson. After being in jail for shooting up a police building, the young man is now being released by an unknown friend." said the man on the news.

"What? How on earth could they let him out!? He's literally a terrible person! Who could be so desperate just to release his ass!?" yelled Zander.

"Maybe it's his foster parents or something," said Liam.

"Ugh, this can't be happening right now."

"Look we don't like what he's done to all of us, but...he is a person after all," said Liam in an honest tone.

"Yeah, a person who's going to destroy us! Guys, this is no longer a good day if he's on the loose. He's after us. I know it. And because I got him exposed to the police, I bet he'll come after me the hardest. Ever since what happened with the girls, he's hated my ass." Samantha grabbed his hand.

"I don't want to make this sound crazier, but... I agree with Zander. Dylan can be seriously dangerous," she said. He stared at her as he looked nauseous.

"Just keep a lookout. Don't let him fool you about anything. He might even have some type of team, so stay low key." Everyone nodded. Although everyone felt like locking away all the doors and

Christopher Martinez

windows, they knew better. You don't run away from danger, but you can't run towards it right away either.

"You think we'll at least make it through graduation?" asked James. Zander gave him a stare as he then shook his head slightly.

"I'm not sure." But Zander was not going to let him ruin anything. This was his year.

It was almost time for the ceremony, and Zander caught sight of Dylan standing nearby. He walked through the huge crowd of people standing around the entrance of the hallway.

"What the hell are you doing here? Are you just asking to get your ass kicked? And who the hell bailed you out?"

"Aw, Z, seems like you've lost your touch," he replied while smirking.

"Look whatever you're planning isn't going to work! This is our graduation day, and you aren't ruining that for me or anyone else out there! Is that understood?" He stared him down.

"Ooo okay man. Look, Monroe High is just a school. I would never do something like that. I've got better things to do." He sounded a little sarcastic.

Zander sat with his classmates in the auditorium and listened to all the speeches. He hadn't been entirely himself as much as everyone hoped. He started smoking occasionally for personal reasons. One of the theories had to be about Dylan. But why distract yourself with such a thing? No one really knew, he was always on his own somewhere and he would never reach out for help.

After a few minutes, the students crossed the stage and took their diploma, but once it came to Zander, his name was announced and a man rushed up behind the microphone.

Perfection Is Key

"EVERYONE EXIT THE BUILDING IMMEDIATELY!!! THERE IS A FIRE SPREADING!!"

Everyone was in a sudden panic as they all rushed out to safety. It was too big of a crowd, the fire moved faster than they did. The building started falling piece by piece. Zander stood near the entrance, making sure there was no one left behind.

"C'mon! Everyone out! Are you guys okay?"

"I hope everyone's out. I hope they're all okay," replied Samantha.

"Where's Ryan?" Zander ran back in as the building started collapsing.

"ZANDER!" yelled Sam. The building fell as Sam started bursting into tears. Zander's parents, along with James and Liam, had comforted her.

Zander walked in weakness while calling out Ryan's name. He couldn't hear anything! Nor really see. He covered his face with his gown.

A firefighter walked up behind him, forcing him back out. He felt awful and scared. His own best friend was nowhere to be seen. He rushed back out as he hugged his friends and parents.

"He's gone. I don't know if he escaped or...or..."

Samantha hugged him tightly.

"I'm so sorry," she said with a small sense of grief.

"Don't worry, I'm sure he is fine. In the meantime, we all need to go home!" screamed Simon, while rushing everyone in the car.

Not only was Ryan missing, so was Dylan. He wasn't seen after the fire had started, nor was he seen heading out. Zander kept track of him sitting in the far-left side, but after the fire, he was nowhere, so it was honestly him who started the whole thing. Or so you would think. At least that was Zander's biggest blame and thought.

Christopher Martinez

It had been a whole weekend, and back on Monday, the gang was called in at the police station for questions about the fire. Zander wondered why they were the only chosen "suspects." But these five stories have secrets. Dylan had plenty of targets, and everyone that rioted against him had a deeper thought on what to do.

"Just because it's my lighter doesn't mean I did it!" said Zander.

"Look, some things just don't go according to plan," said James.

"I swear to you, I'm not lying," said Samantha.

"I don't think I can ever trust myself ever again," said Ryan.

"I guess no one really knows anyone's full story," said Liam.

Forget everything you thought you knew. Monroe High is in deep trouble now. Who started the fire? And why did they do it?

Chapter Twelve
Death of A Dark Angel

Two days ago

The building remained in flames for quite a while. Ryan was the only person on everyone's minds. Zander began shaking in fear because he was so scared to lose his best friend. He wouldn't leave until they found him or confirmed he ran away.

"Zander, we have to leave! Let's just try and call him when we get home," hollered Simon.

"NO! I NEED TO KNOW IF HE'S OKAY!" He tugged on his father's grip, trying to fight his way out. He was aiming to head back into the building.

"I'm sure he is! Let's just go!" Zander suddenly freed himself and ran up to a firefighter.

"Where's Ryan? Can you go in and search for him?!"

"We are sure to tell you if we find anything, but please, stand back and let us handle this fire! It can be very dangerous! You all need to head home and stay safe." Simon pulled Zander away from the scene. Still, he fought and screamed.

Even though the days were looking for a lot nicer, there was no telling what could have happened to Ryan. The faded memory burned still in Zander's mind. And to top it all off, remembering Dylan's disappearance didn't help ease the pain.

Christopher Martinez

It was another warm evening. The Robbins, The Williams, Samantha, James, and Liam waited patiently as the news channel continued with hundreds of stories.

"Son, it's okay. I'm sure he'll be fine. Just breathe and stay calm," said Simon.

"I can't believe this...this is my fault! I left him behind and he's probably dead or knocked out or..." He took a huge gulp.

"Zander, calm down. Breathe. It'll be okay. I promise you. I know he's okay," added Sam.

Zander's patience was running even thinner and there was nothing about anybody or anyone on the news. The newscasters continued speaking about the building burning and were still concerned about what caused the start of the flame.

"Obviously, Dylan did it. He goes for the obvious danger when he seeks real revenge," said Liam.

"What?" asked Zander.

"I mean he was there, right? And I didn't see him after the fire started. And well, he was gone once Samantha grabbed her diploma."

"That is so true," said Samantha as she crossed her arms with a nervous expression. "Guess we should've paid more attention."

"Maybe he just left back home. He didn't look like he was planning anything," said Simon.

"That's how vicious schemers fool you! They seem so innocent until they bring fire starters." He pouted a bit.

"Zander, c'mon. You can't be serious," said Melissa.

"I am. I know it was him."

"You're just overthinking all of this," said Samantha.

"No! Stop siding with them! He is the real villain here! What else could he possibly want with us? If Dylan were the type to move on, he wouldn't even be here in town."

Perfection Is Key

Everyone remained quiet as Zander was so outraged. Without another second, he rushed back to his room.

Samantha felt sympathy and ran after him. And just when you thought things couldn't get worse...Zander patted his pockets and his bags as he realized his lighter was gone. He opened a drawer full of more lighters along with a pack of cigarettes. He pulled one out and lit it as Samantha burst through and caught him. Her eyes widened, but he didn't care. The smoke leaving his mouth like if a ghost came straight out of him.

"What the hell? Are you crazy? You could get killed from those!" She grabbed the cigar and threw it down. He rolled his eyes.

"What's it to you?"

"You know, I didn't want to mention anything, but it sure seems like dickhead Zander's back," she said while placing her hands on her hips.

"Look, this just takes my mind off things for a while! It's not like I'm hurting anyone. Geez, just let me be in peace." Another cigar came sliding out of his pocket.

"Zander...does anyone else know about this?"

"Of course not."

She knocked out the cigar and gripped his arm. She dragged him downstairs, and his fear grew a little. His parents stared at them.

"Everything okay?" asked Melissa.

"Zander has something he needs to tell you all." Everyone remained quiet as they stared at him. He stared at Samantha like she had just exposed an embarrassing photo of him to the whole world.

"No, I don't."

"Yes, you do. Otherwise, I will tell." He dropped his jaw a bit as he lowered his head. He looked angry, yet he knew it was the right thing to do. He then let out a deep sigh.

Christopher Martinez

"Sam... you know I'm not ready to tell them. I need the right time."

"Now is. So, tell them. You'll never get anywhere else if you keep hiding it."

"...okay, for about two weeks already...I've...kind of been...smoking." His parents were in great shock as the boys sat in the same reaction.

"What? Bro, why would you do that?" asked James in a worried tone.

"Cause life got intense and..." He went speechless.

"And what? You should know that this won't cure anything. Don't you remember what I told you about what happened to Dylan when he was obsessed with doing that almost every year? It was a living hell," said James. Zander remained quiet.

"Bro. We're your friends now. We shouldn't start this off with secrets," said Liam.

"Just don't worry about it." The newsman suddenly spoke as he announced a new topic.

"It has just been informed that there was a terrible loss of a young man who did not make it out from the collapsing of the building. Young student, recently freed from jail, Dylan Anderson has been found dead. It all leads back to whatever caused the fire and-..." His voice trailed off. He began to widen his eyes. A quick jump to his eyebrows. *"Oh. Okay. It has just been confirmed that the fire was caused by a lighter designed with a picture of a dragon across it. Police had found this clue near the front of the auditorium."*

They all dropped their jaws a little as Melissa covered her mouth. Zander's eyes widened as he realized it was the one lighter he left behind before starting the ceremony. Samantha rested her hand on his as he stared at her.

"Police have also said that there are five students who knew Dylan Anderson while attending a school in a recently found city called 'Rampage.' The police are having them in for a small survey starting tomorrow."

A while later, the night started growing over the city. The crickets filled the silence while the rattlesnakes shook the fear everyone was holding. A sudden noise ran through their ears as Zander carefully headed slowly to the front door.

    The door suddenly swung open, and Ryan rushed in. Dirt slid out of his hair as he coughed a bit while his face was covered in green smears. Two small cuts laid side to side on his forehead.

    "RYAN!!" He removed his hoodie as Zander helped him over to sit down. "Bro, I thought you were dead!! Why'd you scare me like that? Where were you?" Ryan looked up while breathing heavily.

    "I'm sorry...but I was in such a state of shock, I just ran. I was stuck inside for a little, then I ran out the back door and ran off into this forest looking place until I got out."

    "Did you at least see your parents? They were very worried."

    "Oh yeah, I did before I came here. They know I'm okay."

    "Well...not everyone is...okay," said Samantha.

    "Why?" She then gestured to the screen.

    "Dylan. He's dead. They had announced on the news that he was burned during the collapsing of the building."

    "What the hell."

Christopher Martinez

"And as far as we know, we're at least going to be the one's going into that police station just to be questioned about his death," said Liam.

"They said five though, who else knew him?" asked Sam. Ryan lowered his eyes.

"Duh, me. I mean I'm sure a lot of people would put my name on the list. I may not have done a whole lot with that guy, but... I am good friends with you guys."

"You know what, let's just all discuss this in the morning. We need to rest right now. It's getting late," added Melissa.

It had been two weeks and the day had arrived for Dylan's funeral. His family and other friends stood around as they sobbed and mourned over his casket. The gang felt very awkward standing around, watching everyone shoot dirty looks at them and gossiping behind their backs.

After a while, Dylan was buried. His foster parents absolutely loved him as if he were their own. But above that, Dylan Anderson was a huge jerk and had no heart. But he was still human.

Meanwhile, the gang was living life normally and there were no haunting chills of Dylan or anything. Their lives seemed to be at a steady level. But they each hid something that seemed to be clashing against their kingdom. They were legends. But kingdoms will fall, and no one is safe in Monroe.

One Friday afternoon, the gang spent the time hanging out at the park. Catching up and having a few laughs for the fun of it, but it began to shut down when mouths began stuttering. Ryan's phone chimed repeatedly. Seven messages with a contact named *"Her"* with a kissing face sitting next to it. Zander noticed his phone screen until Ryan snatched it away and placed back into his pocket in a quick rush.

"Uhm, who was that?" asked Zander.

"No one. Random numbers."

"Oh stop! You know you don't have to be embarrassed to tell. C'mon who is she? And why didn't I know about this?"

"Nah man. It's nothing. She's just a friend. Someone close to me back in middle school."

"Apparently *real* close." Everyone teased him, but Ryan had no expression. His face became serious.

"Look I got to go. My mom's having a special family event thing happening and she really wants me to be there. So, catch y'all later." He ran off to his car and sat in it while reading all the messages. He began to write back.

Ryan: *On my way. They don't suspect a thing.*

"He's just being shy. All those crazy nerves jumping around." Zander stopped his teasing as he pulled out his cigar and lighter. Samantha noticed and shoved it out of his hand.

"Seriously? Zander, I thought we talked about this. You know I don't like you doing that stuff when I'm around," she said.

"Babe, it's just a cigarette."

"Doesn't matter! It will end you."

"Yeah? And what if that's my goal!?" She stood in shock. Her head started twisting a bit as she suddenly became dizzy. Within seconds, she was stumbling. Zander held onto her. His eyes staring her down as if she were suspicious of being under the influence.

"You good?" he asked.

"Yeah. I think I just need to eat or lie down. Look, I'm just going to head home. We'll talk more another time." She drove home.

Christopher Martinez

But when she parked in the front, she leaned back and sighed. All she felt was fear. She then turned her head over to her purse. A small stare as she then pulled out the pregnancy test box.

"I'm so sorry," she mumbled to herself.

Back at the park, the boys were just hanging and laughing. It felt nice to be a regular guy. Telling stories about the dangerous skydives, or talking about their future goals, or even remembering dumb decisions whenever they were at a party.

Two random students had walked past them. And one of them took a twisty turn on James.

"Hey you! How's the bang-bang going with Olivia Lovington?"

"What?" He asked while smiling awkwardly.

"Yeah, I heard you two were banging! Tell me, is she as easy to flip as we spoke about?"

"Aha...what? Nah man, I mean you think I'm that desperate?" The boys were amazed at how James could even say that. The two students continued walking with laughs rolling through the distance. James sighed as he then looked back towards Zander and Liam.

"Is that true?" asked Liam.

"It's not. Look, I got to go. I'll see y'all later." He grabbed his fancy set of headphones and headed home. Zander chuckled as he smoked.

"Man, I can't believe how crazy this day turned out to be. But it felt good to get away and just hangout, you know?" Zander said.

"Same. Ugh, I hate that tomorrow is going to be crazier since we have to be interviewed about Dylan's death."

"Ugh, don't remind me." Zander placed his arm over his other while the cigar's smoke slithered through the air.

Perfection Is Key

    Liam suddenly realized the time. The time when his mother would gather all the laundry and wash. This meant going into his room and gathering all the dirty clothes he had lying around the place. Liam was a forgetful person.
    "Ah shit!! I got to head home! I'll see you later man!" He snatched his bag and drove off in a hurry. His wheels screeched like he was sliding on ice.

Liam's mother wasn't a nosy person, nor did she interfere with the privacy of her son, but she noticed a drawer out of the shelf and moved over to put it back in, but something caught her eye, a stack of condoms. She was a bit stunned to see this in his room. But she noticed more, a letter wrapped up in a pair of red underwear. She opened the letter.

'Just a teaser before Friday.' -Jenny Lovington

    She grew in shock as she suddenly heard Liam's running footsteps and him hollering her name. He burst through and stopped in fear as she turned and stared at him. Holding the letter in her hand as she placed the other hand on her hip.
    "Care to explain?" she asked.

Meanwhile, Zander rested on the small table as the wind blew softly against his face. He felt relaxed as he stared up at the sky. The bright sunny day felt like a heavenly place. His phone then rang as he leaned back up and opened the screen to a message from the policeman, Johnny Rivera.

Christopher Martinez

Johnny: 'Interview tomorrow for the case of Dylan Anderson's death. 2:00. Police DP of Lake Monroe!'

Chapter Thirteen
Am I A Suspect?

Zander Robbins
2:00 p.m.

Zander sat in a small room. The camera blurred out until it finally focused on him. Johnny stood behind it, almost like a director waiting for the right moment to yell out 'action!'

"I know it seems odd, but accidents happen, right? I know that I was like a crazy maze to get through, but I can tell you I'm the same person that I've always been," said Zander.

"We just want to know anything you happen to know before Dylan's death. Things like…were you in any relation with this young man? How would you describe it? Little things like that."

Zander rolled his eyes. He stared around the room. Feeling this creepy thought swarm his mind. The memories came rushing back. Every thought. Every word. Every action. Dylan left his mark on everyone he ever knew.

"Well…maybe there's some things I can let off my chest," he continued. Johnny smiled.

FLASHBACK

Zander was worried and angry at Dylan's bail from jail. He believed he was a terrible man walking, no matter what location he landed in. He sat in his room with thoughts on how to ruin Dylan's life sometimes.

Christopher Martinez

Even sometimes wished he would just burn in hell. Especially for all the toxic he poured on everyone. This all happened before graduation.

Before the day that Zander would feel like some successful king, Zander met up with a student behind the building. Little did he know, Dylan snuck up around the corner and watched. All he noticed was Zander trading in some money for drugs. Or so it seemed. Dylan could overhear their conversation.

"Hurry man. Someone could catch us," said Zander.

"Okay. Okay." They traded as Zander walked on, looking around, making sure no one saw him. Dylan hid in a bush. He then rushed up towards the student who was packing things in his backpack. As if he were just told to leave an apartment due to eviction.

"So, what'd you give Zander, huh?" Dylan asked. The student almost crawled up into a ball. He took a step away.

"What? What are you talking about?"

"Give it up. What was it?" Dylan began to tease the kid. Almost poking fun at him. The student shoved him away and ran off. It wasn't much of a getaway. He left a bag behind.

Dylan picked it up. It was an almost heavy bag full of lighters. Why on earth would this kid have a bag of lighters? Could it have been the thing that Zander traded money in for?

Zander spent all day with his bag of who knows what and he would never take his eyes off it. He stayed in the house almost every day. Overtime, Dylan brewed up a small demand on the student to give him whatever he gave to Zander. With the student denying and shoving him away, Dylan's anger grew. With that, he hatched a plan. He was going to kidnap Zander and hide him away until he got his share in whatever the trade was. Why be so desperate over something as small as a lighter? Or could it have been a drug?

Perfection Is Key

Once the right moment came, Dylan found himself sneaking around Zander and captured him. Zander found himself in a dark dusty room, crawling with mice, spiders that hid in the shadows, and broken parts that let sunshine burn through.

"What the hell is this place?! It reeks."

"Deal with it. This place is a great holding cell. And of course, little Z doesn't know how to save himself," said Dylan with a teasing laugh.

"What do you want?"

"Mm... Well, I believe you know what I want. Those drugs that the kid was trading with you! I demand a share!"

"They're just drugs. Nothing special. Sorry to burst that bubble."

"Oh, really!? Aha, seems more like they've been helping your skills in bed! I have some skills too, you know? And if only I can help myself become better with some of my athletic skills, then I can end up on top just as I used to be."

"You don't even have an honest bone in your body. Want skills? Look what I'm working with and just learn. I have a family, my friends, people that I can go to coffee shops and talk with! You know it's never too late to use your powers for good." Dylan paused. The awkward silence ran though. "Look man, they're just pills. Something that'll take my mind off things. Just to calm me down," continued Zander.

Dylan always labeled him as a freakish liar. He believed these pills were improving his skills in everything! Making him some kind of 'god' of the school. Jealousy didn't look good on Dylan. It made him look more scary than usual.

Christopher Martinez

"I demand you give me half! Otherwise, some dirty things are going to come and haunt your ass! You don't want to have to start another war with me, Z. You have no idea what I'm capable of."

"You don't scare me anymore." Though Zander's heart was practically begging to jump out and run away, he knew better than to stand under Dylan's ego.

"Yeah?" He grabbed Zander's shoulders and flung him across the room. Zander felt his head hit against the wall and his back against the chair. He stood up slowly in pain as Dylan grew face to face with him. "Don't forget who taught you how to RUN fear." He stared deep into Zander's eyes with a darkening smirk. It was like starting over. The power of Dylan alone was triggering. He continued. "Now, you want a good graduation? Bring me the pills or I'll just wreck up your pretty boy life and let you rot in my flames."

Zander felt his rage aching in his stomach as he stood in pain. Dylan rolled his eyes and turned to walk out of the room with some sickening pride.

Graduation drew nearer. Families and friends were excited, emotions exploded, and the students were bursting out in joy. The day was in great shape for celebration and achievement. Zander stood in the school with his friends in his cap and gown. His face was neutral, but the anger boiled in his stomach. Samantha stared at him for a little while. Her expression suddenly vanished.

"Hey...are you okay?" she asked.

"Yeah. I'm just...preparing myself you know?"

"Zander, don't lie to me." Her eyes met his as he stared at her in denial.

"I'm not."

Perfection Is Key

"Zander..." she said once more. Her stare now looking a little dark.

"I just have a bit on my mind, but don't worry! Let's just celebrate today!" Their excitement grew once more and headed towards the auditorium. Zander stood towards the back and lowered his head a bit.

Memories of Dylan flooded his mind. The moments when Dylan taunted him, forced him to shatter his own reflection, made him dress and act more 'manly' like him, and even raped his girlfriend! Samantha and Ryan stopped in their place as they stared at him.

"Bro, you good? You've been acting strange lately," said Ryan.

"I knew you were upset! What's going on with you?" Samantha asked.

"Guys, I'm fine. I promise." He whipped out his lighter and cigar as the flame popped out. Their eyes widened as Samantha shoved it out of his hands.

"Seriously!? Okay, first off, we're in the school building! Second, you know that we talked about this! All the pain it causes. All the suffering. Its path to addiction. Don't you see what this stuff is doing to you!?"

"Sam, it's not that bad! Everyone has an addiction that's bad!" Zander snapped.

"Yeah, but it's not something we must have our entire lives!"

"You do you and I'll do me, yeah!?" Ryan jumped in before the conversation could go on.

"Alright! Look man, just calm down. I know smoking takes your mind off some things, but I mean...before walking the stage and having a great celebration? C'mon bro. But if there's something bothering you, you can talk to us." Zander glanced to the side.

"Look, I am the boss of me. I don't need permission from either one of you!"

Christopher Martinez

"Okay. You're not going out there being high," said Sam as she grabbed his hand to try and take away his pack and lighter.

"Hell no," he angrily replied. She could only stare in shock.

"Zander, I'm serious!"

"SO AM I!" She and Ryan freaked at the sight of seeing Zander act this way. Samantha felt a bit of a chill as Ryan felt a bit of some anger.

"A small tip...always think twice about what you say and do," said Ryan. They both walked away as they prepared for the ceremony. Zander remained standing still with a sudden feeling of regret. He straightened his attitude and walked on. Zander was a good kid. Just as he always was. He would never cause a tragedy. At least not by hand.

PRESENT

"I would never set a building on fire," said Zander with an aggressive tone.

"But you seemed pretty furious after what your friends had told you about your smoking habits," said Officer Rivera. "And it seems liked you had quite some grudges to hold onto after what Dylan had done to you in the past, but also in the near future."

Zander stared at him with a serious face. He sat back as he rubbed his hands over his thighs. The sweat began to spread over his palms. His eyes swung back to Officer Rivera who folded his hands in his lap.

"Yes, but I still wouldn't hurt anyone by burning down a building. I'm still a good guy."

Chapter Fourteen
No One Has to Know

James Coleman
2:20 p.m.

James had sat in the same spot where Zander had been. The camera blurred until it was then focused on him. He sat straight as his muscles stiffened through his shirt.

"Of course, I had some issues and secrets of my own. But everyone does, right?"

"I understand that you and Dylan were on a close pact. But I also learned that there were some things that you said that sounded a little threatening," said Officer Rivera.

"Everyone hated Dylan, but no one would hurt him. Especially not by me. Like you said, we were close. I began to hate him overtime, but not enough to make me want to hurt him."

FLASHBACK

James Coleman was a perfect man over at Rampage High and was always taunting Zander. He only cared for one thing. Appearance. Something that involved working out, sports, and just admiring his own body.

Now before Graduation, James had a few run ins with Dylan which made things become a little hectic. Considering they had become frenemies. And Dylan had been recently released from jail. And James wasn't pleased. He sat in the locker room, changing back in

Christopher Martinez

his regular school clothes. Dylan popped in with a wide smile. He stared around the place. The two seemed to be alone.

"Hey there buddy! What's going on? Man, it seems like it's been forever!" James widened his eyes in shock. Yet he felt weird talking to Dylan.

"Dylan...what are you doing here? You know you don't go to school here. If Mrs. Lovington catches you, your ass is dead! People can't even stand to see you roam the streets."

"Ahh c'mon. Just two pals reuniting. Having a little chit-chat."

"Dude, you made my life more miserable than it ever was. Do you ever stop to think clearly on what your actions and words do to others? No, you don't. Because you got such a perfect royal life. I can't even believe that my mind was sucked up into the popular world for over seven years!"

"Oh, boohoo, it's not my fault that other people are living a boring life! I had to make them royals! They valued me. YOU valued me."

"Used to! Liam and I leaving the group was one of the best things we've ever done."

"C'mon man...you know you miss being a ruler of these scumbags! It was like wrapping them up in ropes and swinging them all around!"

"I do not. What I miss is freedom. And now that I got it, it sure feels awful standing next to you."

"C'mon man! You don't ever miss screaming and taunting and teasing people?! I mean, bro, it was our property!! We were gods!!" Dylan's tone turned into rage. The failure was like a punch in the gut.

"...I forgive my old self. I don't care about your ego anymore. Or even how we were gods. Just get out of here before I holler to Mrs. Lovington and watch her throw you out in a blink of an eye." Dylan's face flattened as he felt his anger rise once more.

Perfection Is Key

"P3 will be a no go without you, man. I mean, aha, c'mon you can't be serious about this," said Dylan.

"Leave. I mean it." James never showed fear towards Dylan. All he felt was a desire to tackle him down and throw him back in the little cell. But he knew better now. Dylan slammed his hand against the lockers. He stormed away.

"You're lucky I haven't told anyone about you and that girl." Dylan said with a smirk.

"What...what girl?"

"Don't play dumb...she's pretty cute."

Dylan left with a devious smirk as James lowered his head. Did he know about Olivia?

During a free period, James took Olivia behind the bleachers to talk some things out. He could feel his legs sort of get weak when he was around her, but he kept his cool.

"Are you sure we're alone?" she asked.

"Yes. I promise," he said as he also searched around the area.

"I don't know. My mom can be very sneaky and slick at times. Like that one day when I hung out with some friends at a beach. She played the hot dog stand manager! Gosh, she is so embarrassing."

"Liv, your mom can't reach you here. She's too busy with paperwork." James reached for her hand until she swept it away. "What's wrong?" he asked.

"Um, nothing. I... I just don't want us to be caught. Who knows what could happen to us when we're exposed? There are rumors, gossip, and the worst part is that people could make us look like one of those annoying couples that people think are only wanting sex."

"Babe, we're alone. I already told you this."

"Yeah but-"

Christopher Martinez

"Hey, look at me. I love you. If people want to try and get between us, we'll fight back with more power."

"That's sweet Jay, but there's a lot more evil power that can bash down the good. You know? Sometimes it's just never satisfied."

"Why think so low? We got this. Together."

As she blushed a bit and fell back into his arms, they kissed and started making out. She loved the feeling of her heart drip like crazy over his gorgeous eyes. Dating the principal's daughter was a crazy idea, but James couldn't help himself.

As it was evening, James spent his entire afternoon at the park, relaxing with a book and drink. By the time he decided to leave back home, he walked on by Olivia's house. He always did just to get a buzzy feeling, but while passing, he noticed Liam walking out upon the sidewalk.

"Liam?" He stopped in great shock until he played dumb.

"Hey, what's good?"

"What were you doing at Olivia's house?"

"Huh? Oh, that? Just getting some help on my homework from her mom. You know, since she's a math tutor."

"Mm. Well, was Olivia there?"

"Yeah. Why, you know her?"

"Uh no. Why would you even ask that? What are you, a cop?" His voice cracked as he smiled like an idiot.

"Right. Look man, I got to hit the gym. Do you want to come with me?"

"Uh, nah, man. I'm headed home for some of my own homework to do. But maybe next time." He flashed a smile.

"Okay. Have a good night!" Liam walked on as James felt so concerned about Liam telling the truth. He stared at Liam and then back at the house. He felt okay and he continued walking home. I guess you could say things were steady.

It became mid-week. James and Olivia hung out after school. They spent almost the entire day laughing, flirting, and even making out. She had lied to her mother by saying she would be at the library. But during this beautiful ray of sunshine, it seemed like other clouds like to rain on parades.

As the two lovebirds streamed along the street, a voice interrupted. A young girl with light brown hair. Skin covered in such beauty. Body was magazine thin, yet so curvy. She had beautiful hazel eyes along with a gorgeous smile. She wore a small crop top with a nice shade of blue and sparkle across it. And thin tall heels with glitter and paint patted on them.

"James Coleman. Oh, my goodness! I knew I recognized that handsome, sexy face." Olivia felt uneasy by the sudden words this girl was using. She hugged him as he awkwardly hugged back.

"Kristal! What are you doing here in Monroe? I thought you moved to L.A."

"Yeah, well, my dad did. After their divorce. But I stayed behind with my mom." Within a snap, she made contact with Olivia's eyes and looked her up and down. She was suddenly disgusted with her. Olivia smiled with worry after seeing Kristal's first impression.

"So, this is truly James...but who's the tramp?" Olivia was suddenly offended. James felt a little lost.

"This is my girlfriend, Olivia Lovington. Olivia, this is Kristal. She was my-"

"Actual girlfriend." Kristal interrupted. James sighed as he closed his eyes slowly.

Christopher Martinez

"No. We broke up a long time ago and you just can't seem to leave me alone now."

"ARE YOU KIDDING ME?! WE WERE JUST HAVING A SMALL ARGUMENT!! But we never. broke. up."

Olivia was already feeling fed up with Kristal. She was shallow, a crazy ex-girlfriend who would stalk James almost everywhere he went. Kristal was very preppy. Little short skirt with a big attitude.

"Did you get my present? I sent it to you this morning," she continued with a sudden perk to her smile.

"Present?" James asked.

"Yeah...it's our anniversary?" Olivia began to feel angry. It's like standing in front of a spoiled child. Thinking that just by saying 'please,' then you'll get a free candy. James sure was the eye of it.

"Okay! Look, I believe James decided to choose a better person as his girlfriend. I've heard everything about you and your petty little friends. The best part of the story was hearing about how you all schemed an evil plan against our friend, Zander." Kristal raised an eyebrow at her as she placed a hand on her hip.

"You just don't like the fact that I won this hottie a long time ago," said Kristal as she stepped closer towards Olivia with a dark glare.

"Yeah? I think not. Maybe polish up that attitude of yours and maybe you'll win the war. Because your little win of round one was just a battle." Kristal suddenly closed her mouth as she slightly smiled. She stared at Olivia with disgust. Olivia gave a smirk as she placed her hands on her hips.

"Now just turn your ass around, and leave. For good."

"Hm. Take shelter for once dear. Cause I've been plenty mad." Olivia just held her position as she then smiled.

"Game on." Kristal took a glance at James as she then turned around and walked away.

Perfection Is Key

As it became closer to graduation, James was getting excited. But Kristal had other plans. He headed to the back of the building where she offered him an "apology" bag of cookies. More specifically, drugged cookies. Nothing surprising there. James was drugged after a few seconds. Then everything was slowly starting to fall apart.

"So, this is a nice spot to.... you know," she said as they trailed along the edge of a hill that led to a beautiful lake.

"What? Make out? Because I sure could use some pleasure tonight!" James exclaimed. A giant smile running over his face and they swung their hands like a child strumming along a Disney Park.

"I mean we could. It is pretty romantic. Just like the old times."

With James acting up, he chuckled as he then leaned towards her and kissed her. Which led to making out and a seductive tease. And to no surprise, the two had made love the entire afternoon.

Two hours later, James woke up with a headache and a blanket covering his naked body. He looked around confused with fear and worry. He stood up, put his clothes back on, and ran back home.

He stepped inside. He clicked on his phone. Unread messages from Olivia, Zander, Liam, his parents, and even Dylan. Olivia had left seventy-three messages. While he read her angry words, he looked at Dylan's message next.

Dylan: I knew you were still a freak for her! Hope you had the time of your life man!

A winking emoji sat next to it.

Two photos of Kristal naked on top of him stood under the message as James felt his anger rise. He stared at it for a minute until he dialed his number. He paced the kitchen floor and waited for Dylan to answer.

Christopher Martinez

"Well... I didn't expect you to be my first caller."

"What the hell did you tell Kristal?! I know you are the one who contacted her and told her about me and Olivia!!"

"Bro, c'mon, she missed you and I figured why not get you guys back together."

"You're so fucking demented Dylan! She and our girlfriends were terrible! How could you even think of letting them walk back into our lives!?"

"You seriously need to get laid again- oh wait, you already did! Maybe now you can thank me."

Within seconds, James snapped the end button as the line disconnected. He grabbed his head as he started to overwhelm himself with thoughts. He couldn't go through another stage of being depressed. He finally gained control as he sat by his window, staring out into the streets. Yet his expression seemed furious.

"My turn."

PRESENT

"Sometimes anger can feel better when it has a target. But I didn't kill Dylan. Sure, I was angry with what he did, but I'm not a killer, and I sure as hell wouldn't take it out on him."

Officer Rivera placed a stack of papers onto the edge of the table.

"Hm, well by what I can assume, it sounds like you did. What did you mean by 'my turn'? Did you have any desire to harm him within that moment?" James shook his head as if Rivera didn't know what he was talking about.

"I know how to control myself. I'm not a maniac."

They each stared at him. Rivera then crossed his arms as he stared directly at James' eye.

Perfection Is Key

"We'll let you pass for now. But you're still on my list."

Christopher Martinez

Chapter Fifteen
Threat or Promise?

Samantha Shaw
2:40 p.m.

Samantha was next. She sat anxiously while the vomit nagged in her throat. She felt a bit angry for being considered a suspect. I mean could you blame her?

"I never thought I would have the blood on my hands, but...things just happen," she said.

"Miss Samantha Shaw, I understand that you faked an identity while living in the city of Rampage. And I've also learned that Dylan knew about it and threatened to expose you if you had never let him get whatever he wanted."

"Yes, but after that, he let things go. Eventually everyone found out and it was nothing. So now he had nothing to hold against me. There was nothing I wanted more than to just live life. I wanted Dylan out of my own picture. Not out of the world."

"Why don't you tell us whatever happened between you and Dylan before graduation."

FLASHBACK

Samantha Shaw. The girl that no one knew lived a double life in Rampage. She was a basic girl, wore basic clothing and regular accessories. But at the same time, she was this perfect, glossy barbie upon the halls who made every guy drool and others admire her.

Christopher Martinez

Rampage was perfection. It was not her used to be home. Now that she could be her actual beautiful self, she was living in her own beautiful world, and now she's about to graduate, but before the good days continue, Dylan had other plans in store as always. He was a schemer, a liar, and a fraud.

Samantha strolled downtown to a shoe store and looked at baby shoes. She tried hurrying and peaked around from corner to corner, making sure no one she knew was around. But in a quick second, Dylan appeared in front of her. Her heart almost stopped.

"Whoa! If you wanted to follow me around, all you had to do is ask," he said.

"Ugh, what are you even doing here? Don't you have anything better to do?"

"Ay, I just wanted to come and see you. I know you missed me. Trust me, I've missed you plenty of times." He slid his hand slowly across her hip until she pushed it away.

"Ugh, keep dreaming. I miss you ghosting the town."

"How's the little guy doing?" He placed his hand flat on her stomach.

"What's it to you? It's not yours."

"It could be though. Daddy's going to be gone for a while." Samantha felt disgusted yet a little scared at the same time.

"Just go home. Please."

"Does Zander know yet?"

"Of course not. I'm trying to find the right time. You know what, this isn't even any of your business!"

"So why not tell him now? I think it'd be the perfect time." There went his devious smirk once again.

"Go away!" Dylan brushed her cheek seductively and whispered in her ear.

Perfection Is Key

"Ravishing girls like you are too easy to handle." He smirked at her as she breathed heavily with fear until he then stepped out.

After what felt like forever, Samantha finally headed back home. Zander waited with her mother. She flopped against the door, shoving the bag of items behind her back.

"Zander! Mom...what's going on here?"

"Hey sweetie...uhm, Zander just wanted to stop by and make sure everything was okay. He just seemed a little concerned." Her mother's eyes stared her down. Almost as if they were sending her a message mentally.

"Oh. Well, I'm fine. No need to worry about me!" Zander stood up while adjusting his shirt.

"You sure? Seems like you've been a bit secretive lately," he said.

"I'm not." She began to walk a little faster. But she couldn't get past him.

"Sam. What's going on? What's in the bag?"

"Uh...my mom," she shouted in fear.

"...your mom?" Sam suddenly stood next to her mom.

"She's pregnant!" Her mother widened her eyes as she smiled.

"What? Mrs. Shaw, why didn't you tell us? That's great news!" He was so filled with joy as he hugged her tightly. She laughed while looking at Samantha with a death stare.

It was evening as Zander and Samantha talked. They spent the rest of the day hanging out. But some things went a bit downhill.

"So, how's your mom doing with all the pregnancy stuff?"

"Oh, she's doing okay. It's been a crazy ride so far."

Christopher Martinez

"That's nice. So... why didn't you tell me about her pregnancy? Not to sound harsh."

"Um, I just thought it wasn't the right time. You know? Plus, my mom didn't want anyone to find out just yet either. She intends to freak out a little too much over things like this."

"Hm. I figured she'd at least share with us too."

"Yeah. But that's old news now. Why don't you tell me about school? Hope there's not another P3."

"It's going well. I guess." Zander felt a bit uneasy. It was no help to hear her change the subject in a matter of seconds.

"It'll get better. I didn't like that Mr. Wilson gave us a whole assignment on the Civil War though. I don't think I can study on my own. We should get together this week. I'm sure after that, we can probably get it done early."

"Sure. I guess we could do that." He smiled at her.

"What..." He held her hand as her cheeks began to flush.

"You're just cute when you're nervous."

"Nervous? Why would you think that?"

"Because of your mom's pregnancy... I'm sure it's a little scary, but I know she'll make it. And you will be an awesome big sister." She smiled slightly as she then stared down. He leaned in and kissed her cheek.

"I love you," he said.

"I love you too," she replied. "But I'm not being honest with you." She took a deep breath once more. "My mom's not the one that's pregnant..."

"I knew it," he said. She glued her eyes to his face.

"Wait what?"

"It was kind of obvious. It just wasn't sitting right with me." He let out a small laugh. "Wait...we haven't done anything...so, who's the father?"

Perfection Is Key

"Just don't freak out...but it's Mr. Shue."

Her eyes began to tear up. Zander pulled her into his chest as she closed her eyes and clanged to him.

"Don't worry. I'm here. And your safe now," he said.

It was looking like a late night, and Ryan was walking down the park when he suddenly noticed Samantha behind a tree with her head sort of buried in her knees. She stood up with her tear-filled eyes. He began to walk over toward her.

"Hey, what are you doing out here?" She grabbed her sleeve in her hands as she tried wiping her face.

"Should I ask?"

"Don't. I know it looks bad, but I swear it's nothing."

"You want to talk about it? I'm a great listener."

"No thanks." Her arms were wrapped around her chest as the cool breeze brushed against her face and back.

"Well, do you want a ride back home?"

The two rode on home. They parked in front of her house as they sat back with a heavy sigh. Ryan stared out the windshield for a moment. Dead silence began to fill the air. He turned his attention to her. She shot him a quick glance as she reached for the door handle.

"Um, well, I'll see you tomorrow. Feel better," he said. She stopped and stared at him with such a heavy heart. It was like a bubble grew larger and larger in the center of her throat.

As she remained quiet, she closed the door and breathed heavily. Samantha knew better than to tell people about her dramas, but at the same time, everyone always deserves a friend.

"Look, I have to tell you something, but you have to swear to never tell anyone."

"Of course I swear," he said.

Christopher Martinez

"No, I mean it."

"Sam..." She hesitated before speaking.

"The baby. It's not my mom who's pregnant. It's me." Ryan widened his eyes a bit and sat back up against his seat.

"So, you and Zander...are par-"

"It's not even Zander's..." Ryan then dropped his jaw a bit. He could only think of one other person.

"That bastard! You know what, we'll confront him about all of this, and maybe we can slowly talk to your parents about getting the police too-"

"And it's not Dylan's!"

Ryan sat back and stared at her with a very confused look. There was nothing left to say.

"Then who the hell is the father?"

She just kept staring at him.

Meanwhile, it was officially graduation day and Samantha told her mother she was headed to the Police Station to visit a certain person for a small discussion. Her mother knew who she was talking about. She even offered to attend with her, but Sam declined. She knew it was going to be much better on her own.

She sat with the glass window in front of her and the other seat. The door opened as she heard yelling.

"Oh please! Who in the hell would want to visit me? I'll bet it's some sort of brat!"

"Just shut your mouth, beast boy, and sit down!" The man stared at Samantha. He slowly smirked and took the seat in front of him.

"Hey there princess," he said.

"Don't call me that. You shouldn't even get to speak."

Perfection Is Key

"Ooh back to the old feisty self again huh? I loved playing that little game with you. Made everything a little more fun."

"I told my mother and Ryan about what you did to me."

"Awe. How did that go? Do they want to have a gender reveal party?! That'll be a huge surprise for everyone."

"Gosh, you sicken me. And I thought Dylan was the worst person alive."

"Awe. Well, there's always option number two: abort it. Shit I know I would do it. You don't have to go out and play victim if you don't want it, baby girl."

"Mr. Shue, do you ever stop to think what this will do to me?!"

"Don't you dare play innocent little girl with me! You saw the damn trap and fell right into it! You only have yourself to blame."

She felt pain rage through her bones. But she held back and remained calm. She suddenly slammed the phone back onto its rack and stepped out without a single word.

"Don't go too far! I'll always find your sexy ass," he hollered with a grin as she glanced over at him. The anger burning her eyes.

Sam had enough for the day and wanted nothing more but to be home. Where there was no one and no drama. At least physically. Her phone suddenly buzzed in her pocket. A message.

Busted. She thought. A picture with her and Dylan together. Though she couldn't really tell if the picture was real or edited to look real.

Dylan: *Yup! Yo boy is going to be a daddy soon!*

Sam was furious and felt her fear eating her up like a snake had struck her heel. Her mother walked in, giving her the best comfort.

"Sweetie. Is everything okay? How are you doing?"

Christopher Martinez

She screamed off the top of her lungs. As if someone was holding her voice mute. She burst into tears while collapsing onto the floor and her mother fell and comforted her. Samantha let out her scream, and it felt rather good, but now, she just wanted to cry. She then buried her face into her mother's chest as they each held on. It was a time to be vulnerable. And she had every right to fall.

PRESENT

"Dylan had a bad effect on my life, and I couldn't handle it..." She sort of shook while sitting straight in her seat. Rivera stared at her.

"Well, I'm deeply sorry that you had to go through that. But that seems like enough to have a motive towards Dylan." She lowered her eyes as she played with her thumbs.

"Yeah, I know it does." She then remained silent. Rivera squinted his eyes.

"So, what, are you admitting to killing him?" Her dead eyes stared back at him. She smiled.

"No."

Chapter Sixteen
I'm Not Psycho

Ryan Williams
3:00 p.m.

Ahh Ryan Williams. The charming, handsome, funny, athletic, and crazy guy among Monroe High. He and Zander were the best of friends out of the school. The two did everything together.

Memories that they would never forget. Ryan was almost a perf in Monroe, but not everyone knew exactly what his thoughts were or how he was handling his personal life. And with Dylan in his way, things became just a little hectic. Bonding meant breaking, friends become foes, and perfection was catching up.

"Look, some things just don't go according to plan," he said.

"Mr. Williams, you never personally got involved with Dylan in any way, but I do know that you sought some sort of revenge?"

"That had nothing to do with Dylan. My friend was becoming an asshole. I had to do something. But ever since things went back to normal, I've been doing just fine."

"Tell me your side," said Rivera.

FLASHBACK

Ryan was at home, sipping a nice cup of chocolate milk along with his T.V. blasting sounds of a football game. He sat back on his couch. It was a lazy day at home for him. He was relaxed and calm. Except with all the thoughts and small ball of anger towards Dylan's release.

Christopher Martinez

Meanwhile, Dylan was at home in this small room with computers and other kinds of technical devices. He typed and scanned around every screen with his daring glares and devious thoughts.

He hacked into Ryan's phone. Every message shown under the contact's name, *'Her'* seemed very...odd.

Jared: Dylan being unleashed was so unfair! He should've stayed there!

Kendall: Dylan should never be trusted!

Cullen: He's such a bad influence on this town. He's got to go!

Ryan: What if we killed him?

Ryan had never been the type to attempt murder or even think about it. But this aggravated Dylan and made him question why they discussed this whole stupid idea. But it didn't stop him from fighting back.

Within a quick second, Dylan stormed off to Ryan's place. He banged on the door with his full force and knocked continuously and obnoxiously. Ryan suddenly answered and his face dropped.

"Ugh, what are you doing here?" Ryan asked.

"Just wanted to drop by before I pound your face in!!"

"Excuse me?"

"You and your little buddies think you've got everything under control huh?! Think twice."

"Look, let's talk about this somewhere else, yeah?"

"Oh no, you like the attention, don't you? You're an attention grabber!!"

"So, what if I am? Everyone enjoys it much better than when it's on you."

Perfection Is Key

"Well, they may not have a problem with it, but I DO!"

Dylan suddenly shoved Ryan across the floor. He picked him up and pinned him against the wall while his eyes raged. Ryan and Dylan were the same body type, so he had no problem handling him with a fist and knee.

Eventually the fighting stopped. Ryan held onto his head for a moment.

"Look, I wasn't going to agree with any of the guys to try and 'rid' you of the city, but... you got to understand that everything you've done to half these people is not just another disaster. Having you on the loose means you could do more or worse," said Ryan.0

Dylan lowered his head as he sighed.

"I know that I've done a lot of stupid things in the past. I know that I can be sneaky, but I swear, I am working on this shit. But too many times, no one has bothered to spare my feelings and think about what I'm going through!"

"All the toxic you spread upon my best friend and his fellow mates including your own wanabes, it left them in such pain. You don't even know what it's like to be the victim of someone who literally holds power over you man." Dylan began to think.

"You know, it does make me wonder though... How is Zander handling all this group chat stuff? Is he in on it too?"

"...he doesn't know. He doesn't know a lot of things."

"Hmm, what a pleasant surprise. Can't wait to see his reaction when I tell him."

With that, Ryan was suddenly angry again and pinned Dylan up against the wall once more.

"Oh, so now Mr. Perfect is going to go and pour more toxic after saying he is working on his bad side? I knew you were a piece of shit!!" Dylan shoved him off as he headed back out of the house.

Christopher Martinez

"I'll be back. You just wait and see what I have in mind. You're messing with a king boy. And now you got to face his wrath."

"Over my dead body." The door slammed shut.

Ryan stared around and began to think. He then opened up the group chat and began texting once again.

Ryan: So, what's the plan?

Cullen: How about on Graduation Day? Let's tie him down and then beat him up till he dies! We can make it look like an accident.

Kendall: On graduation? I can already imagine how happy everyone would be.

Jared: Kill him, then place his body in the back of the building and let others deal with it. Make sure to leave no evidence. Wear gloves, masks, and no skin.

Ryan was going with the suggestions. Though a lot of times, he had second thoughts. He walked over toward the kitchen and poured out a little wine. He looked around his counter which had about fifteen empty bottles of alcohol. He was personally an alcoholic. One who enjoyed drunkenness to its fullest. Another secret hidden away from his own best friends.

While Ryan was drinking the night away, Dylan took more steps ahead and headed over to Zander's house. He already took screenshots and even printed out copies of the messages just for any case. He was going to show Zander some truths about Ryan.

As Zander opened the door, Dylan stormed in with flared eyes.

"Guess what! Your little bestie has some juicy secrets of his own! Surprise surprise."

Perfection Is Key

"Excuse me? What the hell makes you think you can just run in my home and make up such an idiotic story?"

"Idiotic? Then explain this." He handed the phone to him. Zander read through the messages as if it were staring at a picture of a pedophile who had just been arrested.

'Her' was revealed to him as a group of guys who were attempting to murder Dylan without any hesitation. Zander suddenly stopped as he let his brain get caught up in the web of overwhelming thoughts. He noticed the names upon the group chat.

Jared Jones, the super strong football player who is the main star of the squad. Cullen Swan, the leader of the drama club who intends to make every girl drool and screech at his passion of acting and being a charm in general. Kendall Walker, the charming artist who can draw out all of anyone's flaws and turn them into masterpieces.

Girls crush on them hard, and guys admire their skills. Zander was suddenly hit with every little bad memory he had.

The taunting, the mean kids who trashed his soul, the mean teachers who publicly humiliated him, P3, the building's mockery, and just...the perfection. He looked up at Dylan.

"Thanks for sharing. I'll talk with him about this. Just don't do anything stupid."

"No promises," he said unamused. He then grabbed the phone and headed back out. Zander gave a stare as he sat in pain suddenly.

Ryan still texted the group even if Dylan was secretly watching. He didn't care at all. It's like all the messed-up things in his head were breaking down the walls he built up.

Fast forward to a couple of months, and Dylan had a great amount of power once again. Ryan's secret group was slowly starting to fall apart. And his secret was now standing on the edge of the cliff.

Ryan: *Guys c'mon. This isn't time for silly games.*

Christopher Martinez

Jared: Nah man. You lied to us. You just wanted to use us for some money! Just for you to take the credit of riding Dylan out of this town? No way, I thought we were a team.

Ryan: We are...guys, don't listen to Dylan. He doesn't know what he's talking about. He's the one trying to rebuild Rampage out of Monroe. Don't let him!

   Dylan was beginning to gain control. He had people with twisted thoughts and poisoned minds all over again. He weaved a huge web once more with a very unbalanced trust. No surprise there. The web was so thick, you couldn't even move if you were caught up in it.
   Overall, the gang not only turned, but threatened Ryan about his drinking problem in front of the whole school on graduation day.
   Filled with rage, Ryan had his plot set and ready to fire. It became night as Ryan snuck into the school with two beer bottles. Not filled with beer, but with gasoline. He set them upon a table in the auditorium. The stage was decorated with graduation cups, plates, balloons, and even a few gifts.
   A sudden creek and Ryan looked over his shoulder to see a small part of a black hoodie figure exiting and the door slowly closing. He walked over in a hustle and peaked out into the hallway. But there was no one standing or walking among the halls. He searched for a good five minutes.
   Shoes were squeaking, doors were slamming, material was falling, and the lights were flickering. Ryan was just going to forget it as he hurried along back to the room. He knew he had someone watching him, but there was nothing that was going to ruin his plan. Sometimes, Ryan felt like he was the protector of his friends. And he would do anything to make sure they were living a happy life.

Perfection Is Key

Unfortunately, things seemed to become a bit unplanned for Ryan. As he headed back into the auditorium, a sudden scent ran up his nose. The smell of gasoline. He then caught the side door closing. The dimmed lighting barely made the room visible. He suddenly turned his attention to the floor.

Both beer bottles were shattered against the wall and no scent or sight of gasoline anywhere.

"Oh shit!" he screamed in a whisper. The creepy feeling of having someone watch you and do your dirty work for you was not the best thing in the world. Ryan rushed out to his car and drove away.

PRESENT

"Okay so you admit that you brought two bottles of gasoline to the auditorium. But only because of what your gang friends did?"

"Yes. Dylan had exposed me, but, I promise, I didn't set it off."

Rivera sat back in his seat as he stared at the other two officers and detectives in the room.

"Okay. You'll only be released this time, but make it count. I don't want to have to have you back in here." Ryan stood up as he swung his jacket over his shoulders.

Christopher Martinez

Chapter Seventeen
Always Hidden

Liam Dixon
3:20 p.m.

Last, but never least, Liam Dixon. The full-on fashion designer who could make anyone look like they just shopped from an expensive store that had material that seemed uncommon. Liam was creative, a model, an athlete, and just pure perfection. He was his best when doing his worst, but this is a new Liam now and all he cared for was peace, yet still loved creativity. Just trying NOT to take advantage and make others look like him. He sat in front of the camera.

"If I wanted to be a murderer, I would've torched the place a long time ago," he said.

"Liam, you were also a member of the P3 group which involved Dylan. And I know that you quit being his friend as well. Don't you think there was somewhere along the line, that maybe you thought of harming him?" Rivera asked.

"Yeah. I mean I have nothing personal against him, but I did hate how he acted and who he was sometimes. He became a controlling man."

"Apparently he did strike out at you." Liam lowered his eyes as he began to think.

FLASHBACK

Christopher Martinez

Liam and a few other students, along with Principal Lovington, stayed over in the auditorium after school to decorate a few tables for Graduation.

"Okay, Mike, put those flowers on the edge. Tammy, make sure all the tables are perfectly covered. And Kim, go and set up all the centerpieces and make sure they are in great position," said Mrs. Lovington.

They each began scanning through everything to make sure it was in great shape for the next day. Liam moved around so much that he knocked over a vase. Tammy began to sweep as some of the jocks snorted at him.

"The hell. You trying to ruin everything before we even start?" teased one of the guys.

"It was an accident. Alright?" Responded Liam with a confident tone. Principal Lovington stared at him.

"Liam, we need to talk." She then gestured toward her office. They each stepped in. His heart sort of rushed and Lovington leaned against the edge of her desk.

"Please shut the door." He slowly closed it. His eyes suddenly met with hers. Time almost felt as if it stood still for a moment.

They could suddenly feel the tension rising between them. They rushed into each other and started making out. The burning desire between them. They were always trying to be inseparable! Liam knew the consequences once things went a little wrong, so they would try their absolute best to keep things on a low, but 'good' things don't last forever.

A while later, throughout the day, Liam ended up in Mrs. Lovington's bed. They laid together in silence as her head and hand were right upon his chest. He then broke the silence.

Perfection Is Key

"I know this is something not to be worrying about, but..."

"Ugh don't even. I know what you're going to say and I'll admit, I've been feeling the same way." She rubbed her thumb over his soft skin.

"Really? So, what should we do about it?" She remained silent as Liam could tell what she was thinking. "I don't want to pressure you on this," he continued.

"...Liam, you're a great student, but I'm your principal, and I know this relationship seems so amazing, but it can't last. It's just not right. I mean, the real question here is why do we keep doing it? Acting like nothing is wrong here."

"You don't think we should stay together?"

"It's just not something we should keep up. Sooner or later the students, the boarder, the other teachers, and even family will find out and it's going to turn to chaos. Things will get hectic, and I could get fired immediately. So, I'm sorry to tell you this, but...this has to stop."

Liam understood what she was saying, yet he felt sad. He couldn't seem to understand why he was grieving since he knew what he got himself into and that it was all wrong. He knew what the world would say. He grabbed his clothes, put it all on, grabbed his belongings and stood at the entrance of the bedroom door.

"I love you," he said. She smiled at him as he headed out and started walking along her sidewalk. He looked around, making sure no one he knew would catch him. As he hurried along, he heard a familiar voice from behind.

"Liam?" He turned his attention back. He caught the smirk of a familiar face. He smiled like a crazy person, almost giving himself away.

"Hey James. What's good?"

"What were you doing at Olivia's house?"

"Huh? Oh, that? Just getting some help on my homework from her mom. You know, since she's a math tutor."

Christopher Martinez

"Mm. Well, was Olivia there?"

"Yeah. You know her daughter?"

"Uh no. Why would you even ask that? What are you, a cop?" His voice cracked as he smiled like an idiot.

"Right. Look man, I got to hit the gym. Do you want to come with me?"

"Uh, nah, man. I'm headed home for some of my own homework to do. But maybe next time." He flashed a smile.

"Okay. Have a good night!" Liam walked on as James felt so concerned about Liam telling the truth. He stared at Liam and then back at the house. He felt okay and he continued walking home.

This was the moment where James weaved a huge web, while Liam was the fly who was stupid enough to fly into it. But at the same time, he knew exactly where he was headed.

Now we come back to the moment when Liam forgot about time, ran off back home, and ran into his room to find his mother looking at her hands which were filled with a stack of condoms and a love letter from Mrs. Lovington.

"Care to explain?" she asked.

"Mom, I know this is strange to hear and see, but I swear this is nothing. I mean, it's not a huge deal. I can promise that."

"Not a huge deal? You think just because you have all the glam in the world, and the kids are still admiring you for a perfectionist that you can run off with some tramp? Especially a principal?"

"Whoa take it easy now. Mrs. Lovington is a nice woman, but you have nothing to worry about because we broke up and stopped all of this little mess."

"Oh wow." Her sarcastic tone was firm. "Okay, then good. Why have all these condoms? Were you guys having hookup nights?"

Perfection Is Key

"No! Of course not."

"Liam Dixon!" The chaos was rising everywhere. Liam was losing control with every relationship he had by either friends, family or even people. Life can get messy when it comes to trying to get away with little dirty secrets.

"I promise you we didn't." His flaring eyes were telling her another side of the story.

"Gosh, I thought I raised you better than that!"

With anger and disappointment, his mother stormed out of the room. He sort of felt annoyed. But there was a sense of regret building in his stomach. Sometimes the spell may last, but there's never going to be a bigger jar to hold it all.

Another Thursday and Liam was sitting down for lunch with his thoughts stressing his mind. His phone suddenly rang. He jumped in his seat.

"Hello?"

"GET OVER HERE TO THE OFFICE YOU SHITHEAD!! WE HAVE SOME THINGS TO DISCUSS!"

The line died as Liam stared at his phone in confusion. He headed on down to the office where he found Mrs. Lovington, James, Olivia, and Dylan. James was filled with rage. Pacing the floor back and forth. The negative vibe was very noticeable.

"Is there a problem?" Liam asked.

"DUH! You told her that Olivia and I were dating while you were hoeing around with her on her own property! So now, she's forbidding me from ever seeing her again!!" James screamed his feelings off the top of his lungs.

"Now wait a minute," said Lovington in a demanding tone.

Christopher Martinez

"I just thought you and Kristal were getting back together. Considering she had come back to town and was wanting to get back together with you," said Liam.

"Well, what an idiotic move for this chess game!"

"Says the one who made the move of sleeping with the daughter!" James stared him down as he went speechless.

"You know, I'm just disgusted at the fact you two were sleeping together. I mean, what kind of person does that?!" said Olivia.

"Look, it's nothing now. Why is this such a big deal? So, people make mistakes. So what?" Liam raised his arms in defense.

"You're forgetting she's my mother!" Olivia screamed.

"Watch that mouth young lady!" her mother screamed.

"Why should I!? You obviously didn't when you were out and about with him!!" Dylan laughed at what he heard.

"This is almost just too good to watch," he said.

"Dylan, you're just a piece of shit. You think you can just put your nose in everyone's business, huh?" screamed Liam as Dylan stared at him with a grin. Dylan honestly was trying to be a good-hearted student, but it just never lasted more than a second.

Chaos grew and relations broke hard. Dylan was officially expelled. But still attempted to go to graduation.

It was finally night. Liam was so tired of everything; he had the thought in his head. He sat in silence. With his mother fully asleep, he headed on down to the school. He turned into a darkened area a bit far from the entrance. He noticed another vehicle parked in the front.

As he headed inside, he saw no one nor heard anything. All he saw was the regular old school sitting in darkness. He suddenly caught sight of a young man walking into the auditorium. He followed and stared at him. He tried figuring out who he was and why he was there. But the man would not show his face.

A sudden thud to a trash can. A loud crash and sound. Liam hurried away behind a wall as the guy snuck around the whole building trying to see who was there with him. He hollered and hollered. Liam snuck into the auditorium. Two beer bottles sat on the floor near the side of the doors. He inhaled as he smelled the scent of gasoline from the bottles. Before he could do anything else, a sudden voice spoke.

"What are you doing here? You shouldn't be here. This is not your fight, Liam."

A young student dressed in a black hoodie knocked him out. They grabbed the bottles and poured the gas around the edges of the walls. And after they were done, they shattered the bottles against the wall. They dragged Liam into his truck and left him there as they drove off.

As of now, we do know that Ryan was the man who brought the bottles. As he came running back to find them shattered, Ryan caught sight of a bracelet and an earring. He recognized them both.

"Samantha? Why would she be the one following me around?" he said to himself.

Liam suddenly woke up to find himself in a hospital bed. The plain walls almost brought sadness from everyone. The T.V. on loud volume and his mother sitting nearby. He could feel a sudden small headache. His mother smiled at him.

"Hey sweetie... you're awake. How are you feeling?"

"Fine, I guess." He pushed himself up to feel comfortable.

"That was some crazy drunk driving you did last night. But the doctor says you're going to be fine. And so, after tonight, they're going to release you and we can go out for lunch." She held onto his hand as

Christopher Martinez

she then smiled once mor. He stared around the room one last time. All he could think about was everything. He felt confused. What did she mean drunk driving? Liam would never be that person.

"What are you talking about?" he asked.

PRESENT

"I guess no one really knows anyone's full story. And it may take a while for a person to get out of a trap. But they only take action if they truly desire it." Liam was remaining in his safe spot. No more going out, no drama, no more tragedy.

"So, you don't remember what happened after getting hit in the head?" asked Officer Rivera.

"No. I wish I did. My mom always tells me that it had to do with that drunk driving, but...I can't help but think that she was told wrong." They each stared at each other as the tension built.

"Alright, you're free. But if anything comes up that you can remember, call us back and we can go from there." Rivera then stared at the other officer that stood in the room with a folder and binder in her arm.

"Now we just need to know who was in that hoodie," he said.

Chapter Eighteen
It's All Over

If you could be labeled as anything in a school, what would it be? A jock, a loser, a freak, an artist, or even just...a perf? What if life suddenly turned upside down, weirder than usual, and gave its worst road that had more than bumps and cracks? Places can be scary to walk into nowadays. Zander Robbins was nowhere near anyone or anything normal. Normal was completely dead for him. Rampage ripped his soul out and made him their paper doll. I'm sure all of us can relate in some sort of way.

    Some souls can be dark. Others are light. A few can appear as sweet, but there's a mask that's always found upon them. Some souls can rule kingdoms. Others being followers and wanabes. Who wants to live in a world that believes in pure perfection about everything and everyone? I know I wouldn't. At least wished I hadn't.

    The rest of the following is a bit intense. Some things can go horribly wrong for so many people. And revenge is never an answer, but it can really pick at one's heart. And in the end, things can turn to ash really quick.

After the small argument with Samantha and Ryan, Zander pulled out one more cigar and lit it up. The ceremony was about to start as the smoking calmed him down. After finishing, he headed over quickly to a small room filled with jackets, backpacks, brushes, combs, cologne, perfume, shirts, earphones, and shoes. It was where all the students kept their belongings. Zander placed his lighter on top of his backpack

Christopher Martinez

and hurried along back. Little did he realize; he left the door standing wide open.

As for James, he had the whole Kristal issue going on. After seeing what Dylan posted about the two, Olivia and he were separated for days, while he and Kristal were also getting in the way of every little thing. With a heart of hate, James grabbed a lighter of his own and headed over to Kristal's house with a bouquet of flowers. He set them down by the door and set them on fire. He then attached a note.

'Hell's headed your way, bitch.' -James

Now Samantha was not going to be cheerful with all the crap she's already been through. And with Dylan calling himself the father of her child was a big no no. She stormed into his house.

"You want to tell me why you're being such an ass again? I mean what, you think just cause you're some charming douchebag, you can do whatever the fuck you want?! You know what, don't even answer that."

"Whoa, whoa, now calm down little kitty cat. You don't want to scare the mice away."

"Please. Even they would be better off without you."

"Awe, Sam. Is there a bother going on for you? Cause…I could probably make it better." He began to slide his hands upon her hips. She shoved him away.

"Get your disgusting hands away from me!! Let's just get something straight, YOU are not cut out to be a father nor will you ever be!! So, don't even think that you can just step on up and take a bow for a price you never earned."

Perfection Is Key

"Let me tell you something, you guys were the reason why I became the way I am. Of course, just worse. You see, before all this stupid disaster, I had a whole world that would bow to me and worship me. I used to be a king! And then you people ruined it with your coming and changing of Rampage!! It may look like you got rid of it, but you really didn't. You and your little crew have no idea what I'm capable of." His glaring eyes almost sent shivers down her spine.

"Awe, boo hoo! We made a difference with Rampage and kicked it on out of here! Everyone actually cheered when you landed in jail. I mean, trust me when I say this, Dylan, but I thought it was the best thing I had ever seen. But then to watch you and your father squirm because you didn't get your way? That definitely topped it."

"I gave everything to everyone! Until Zander came along. Then Ryan hacked the systems to reveal secrets, you played double trouble, and James and Liam abandoned me for you lame asses!! Luckily though, the future you each hold, is in great danger."

"You can blow out all the candles you want, but your wish will never be my command." Samantha was disgusted at what she was hearing. The fear she had towards Dylan grew once again.

He paced the room around her with a malice smirk and stare. Her reaction was so satisfying to him. This is exactly the one moment where Dylan could wrap her mind in such a strong rope that it squeezed out all the thoughts of what to do or who to go to.

Meanwhile, Ryan had run home after noticing he was caught in sight at the school and that the gasoline was gone. While preparing for graduation, he and the students stood behind the front doors and spoke amongst each other. A sudden holler to his name.

"Ryan! May I speak to you really quick?"
"Yeah coach! What's up?"

Christopher Martinez

"Listen. I know it's really none of my business, but you mind telling me why you were here last night?"

"Wh-what? Coach I mean whatever you saw, it was noth-"

"Don't even bother alright? I understand you were probably going to miss Monroe High and so you came down just to look around once more huh?" Ryan's heart dropped like a saggy bag of beans.

"Right! You're so right." Coach Vega was Ryan's all time favorite coach for the four years of his high school career. He sarcastically laughed with him over the assumption of Ryan being there. Ryan loved Monroe High, but he thought that burning it would help it from ever becoming Rampage due to Dylan's return.

"Well, all I can say is...I'm so proud of you. You have honestly been one of my honored students who worked diligently and put his all! You made the team better and stronger! We made it through the year with full strength and integrity. Don't stop that. You are stronger than you know." Ryan and Coach chuckled at each other as he left with a thinking mind.

Liam was still kind of lightheaded over the night being knocked out. Until suddenly...

FLASHBACK

A sudden voice spoke.

"What are you doing here? You shouldn't be here. This is not your fight, Liam." He widened his eyes.

"Dylan?" He punched him to the ground and knocked him out. Liam then woke up in the hospital bed as his mother smiled at him.

"Some drunk driving you had last night."

Perfection Is Key

PRESENT

Liam stood quietly with the process of the hoodie man's identity running through his mind. The visions blurred when he tried to remember. He suddenly overheard a conversation between James and Samantha.

"I know right? I mean cause like who would even bother going into so much trouble just to try and rob a school? Or even like burn it?" said Sam.

"You guys know about that? How?" asked Liam.

"Yeah, I mean everyone knows about it. It was pretty creepy to hear that someone could just come on in and possibly set bombs all around the place," said Sam.

"I'm surprised he didn't even bother to steal anything. I mean, this school is elegant. Not Rampage elegant, but you know," said James.

"It was really scary...," said Liam in a shaky voice.

"What do you mean?" asked Sam.

"...the hoodie man...it was scary seeing him there and knocking me down."

"Whoa. Wait, you were there?" asked James.

"Yes, and I remember seeing him. His face."

"Then who was it," cried James.

"Dylan." It was so pressured upon his mind, and the pain of his knockout was too intense for him to properly process. He remembered seeing him and speaking to him. So now, the only real question is...why would Dylan Anderson, an all time adored 'god' who tortured Zander and his wanabes and considered himself the ruler of all rules and king of all kingdoms and walked out of jail with an even more demonized pride, want to burn down a building?

Christopher Martinez

Now sometimes, we can think that the obvious is there. But are we sure?

Whatever reason it was, it didn't end well. Obviously, he wanted revenge. Revenge with flames. We have all come to know who Dylan was. Except, did we ever know WHY?

What I'm about to reveal, is a story that many have heard and seen. Every time it is unleashed to the public, reactions of shock and amazement turn to grief. Dylan Anderson had more than just a vain soul. He had a story. Here's that story.

Dylan sat at home with a book opened on his bed. His foster parents always enjoyed seeing their child with a book. His top genres were sci-fi and action. His passion for reading was something he never liked to admit. He was in love with his skill of reading and using great grammar.

"Sweetie, James and Liam are here to see you…" He then would hide the book and change his clothes and put on his attitude. He would say hi as he opened the door to James and Liam while his mother would accidentally reveal things. Things that would spark Dylan's anger.

"Honey, I'll go put your books in your room."

"Aha, mom… C'mon you know I hate books. They'll rot my brain, I don't want to be a nerd! Remember?" Her smile would sort of fade with his hurtful words, but then again, she was used to it.

Now before I tell you more, I must reveal what truly happened the night of the fire. As far as we've been informed, Dylan was the hoodie man. He poured the gasoline everywhere. Why though? Because of all the stress and pressure and complicated issues between him and others, he was officially done with life. He didn't have true parents growing up and had a lot more to his life than we know.

Perfection Is Key

Kristal had informed other students that Dylan was sneaking towards the back of the stage. She questioned it and felt a bit worried. Obviously, he had taken the lighter that Zander had put with his belongings and through it on the gasoline. The fire started as everyone panicked. Which we all know now.

Sadly, Dylan remained behind as he stood front and center of the stage and let the fire burn his flesh. He screamed off the top of his lungs as he burned to death.

So, what was Dylan's life like? Why would he commit suicide?

Dylan Anderson. Gone too soon. He too, was a victim.

Christopher Martinez

Chapter Nineteen
I'm Not Afraid of Anything

Dylan's Backstory

Dylan Anderson was once a child too. A child who was cheerful and playful. He would play outside with his friends and get super creative when it came to doing activities involving arts and crafts. But not only did he have the good, there was of course, the bad. Dylan's original parents were a young couple who made a lot of stupid decisions. Just like most couples nowadays.

They intended to take the risk of having a child. And once she gave birth, she did not desire him nor did his father. But only because his father didn't feel ready. His real father, who we know is Mr. Shue began talking to him again by the age of thirteen. Mr. Shue was an abusive father. Emotionally anyway. His foster father was the physical one. Not so much with Dylan being raised the way he wanted to be.

"Dad, why does everyone pick on me about not playing sports? I mean, I'm not ready for tough sports, even you know that," said Dylan. His father ended up socking him against the head.

"You want to know something? They have all the rights in the world to pick on you! You want to be a wuss the rest of your life?"

"Well, no-"

"Then suck it up and open up your damn sore eyes! The world can only be unicorns and rainbows for girls. Not for MEN!!"

Throughout his whole life, Dylan never got to see or meet his mother. She died in a car accident when he was 15. His foster mother grew really close with him. But when it came to his fathers, it was a

Christopher Martinez

whole other level. Tension grew all the time between the two. A true home is one of Dylan's deepest wishes. But one that seemed impossible to achieve.

There'd be moments when Dylan and his dad would have constant arguments. Dylan was not even into any kind of sports as a child. He hated playing rough when it came to sports. He would play out with his father and as he would toss the football, Dylan would get a bit scared and not catch it. With that, his father would walk up to him and grab him by the shoulders and come to his face.

"Is this what I taught you? To be a scared little boy? I think not!"

"I'm sorry. It just comes too fast for me. I'm still getting used to it."

"Bullshit!! You either grow some balls and face the consequences of being a man, otherwise, you'll just be ugly and boring!! Be a man!! No one wants to see a weak little boy who has no future!" They'd continue playing and Dylan would be uncomfortable.

But he was forced into so many things that it would haunt his memory forever.

By his teen years, Dylan was experienced in so many tragedies that it had made him the biggest asshole we all knew. At least, that's what the world would call him. He would stay home reading a few books, tossing his football around, and even sometimes help his little foster brother build some crafts for certain class projects. He was like this little angel at home, but when it came to being out in public, he was the demon that we all knew.

"Dylan, I need help on something. We have to do a poster that describes us, but I have no idea how I want to design it. Have any ideas?"

Perfection Is Key

"Hmm, it seems like you could throw on some layered patterns with some more colors. You have your interests and people who inspire you, but it needs designing and color. And I'm sure you'll end up with an elegant piece of work."

"Are you sure?"

"Yeah man, totally. Don't let others tell you otherwise. This is about you. Not them." With his kind words and motivation, his little brother would take the risk and embrace his creative side and stand his ground for those who disliked his ideas.

It would come down to waking up in the mornings and putting on his shirt that had some sexual tease or some ugly beast on it. Then he would brush his teeth and play around with his beautiful hair. Then he would get a shaving knife and cut off every zit or blackhead he had, big or small, to make sure his face looked perfectly perfect.

Dylan thought of Zander as a true person. One who had a big heart and carried so much kindness. He honestly envied Zander. By coming to know Zander more personally on his own time, Dylan grew more in his comfort zone. It was like going back to his child years with his dad. Zander made Dylan laugh here and there and he would sometimes inspire Dylan to do something with his own life.

There was a time when Zander was just screwing around in his locker as Dylan approached him.

"Such a pity that this locker holds your unimportant belongings. It makes me sad to see how poorly you live."

"Dylan. Why are you such a jerk man? I get that perfection is your number one title, but why take out some hate and throw it upon others like they're some kind of...peasant?"

"What I spread is not hate. It's truth. I'm what everyone wants to be and I'm everyone's type. Take notes buddy."

"Nah man. You want the truth? Hear this... When you first saw me, what exactly ran through your mind? Ugly, terrible, rachet, awful,

Christopher Martinez

trash... you see, Dylan, you have a black heart that just won't go back in its cage. You wanted revenge and hate and evil upon others lives. There were nasty rumors, black butterflies, and grave darkness that destroyed the beautiful city of Rampage." Dylan stood back a bit with no expression. He remained silent as he continued listening to Zander.

"I know what you went through when you were a child. James and Liam told me. They didn't know everything and neither do I, but the fact that I've heard enough to know about what happened with your father and how you became a foster child and the abuse and all the other things. And truly, I wanted to help you, but you never let me and never wanted help or happiness. You were too busy blinding yourself from true love in the world." Dylan felt a bit embarrassed yet managed to stay silent. Zander suddenly noticed Dylan's eyes tearing up. He knew he could change and be a better version of himself.

"...you know you can become better and help me make a difference, but...real question is...are you ready to drop all the obstacles in your path to freedom?"

Dylan and James were, of course, the best of friends at Rampage. The two had taunted others and made everyone around them feel super scared for life. It's like they were these so called "rulers" of the school. Which is what they considered themselves throughout those years. Now that James hates Dylan, things between the two have gotten awkward and non-friendly. Dylan would try his best everyday after school or randomly on his own, trying to take James back as his friend and make him change the way he looked at him, as the greatest douchebag that could ever live upon this earth.

"Hey James!" James would notice him and roll his eyes.

"What are you doing here?"

"Just listen to me for a bit, please. Give me five minutes."

Perfection Is Key

"...four."

"Bro, I know I've messed up so many times, and you can name off a whole entire list, but man, I don't want to keep making these mistakes. I need my best friend back."

"Dylan, you were never there for Liam and me. It's like you didn't have a phone to hit us up and say let's hang out or go to the movies. We were your wanabes. Your slaves. The guys that others feared and idolized yet never got to the level. I think back at it all and I hate it. I wish I were never in that position! Wishing I could redo the whole thing, but I'm glad it changed me instead and made me realize what life is really about."

"I know...I'm beginning to think the same thing."

"So, you want to become someone better? Face the facts, perfection is never the key." He walked out as Dylan stopped him.

"Alright! So, it's not. I'll look at everything and everyone as a valued piece. I'll change and start using more kindness. Please, just give me a chance." James felt the sympathy. But he also learned to never actually wish harm on someone or wish death. But he did know how to trust and who to trust.

"Make it worth it. I know you can change. But when it's confirmed, come find me. Otherwise, have a good day. See you around man." Dylan suddenly felt his guilt and hurt go away slowly. He stood in silence as he also managed to bring himself back up and act on James' words.

Samantha Shaw always had hate towards Dylan. Ever since he taunted and bullied and shattered the souls of the good, she's hated his attitude and his personality in general.

Sam was just walking down a sidewalk as she then stopped by a coffee shop. While walking in, she noticed Dylan talking with some

Christopher Martinez

other student at a table. He noticed her and gave her a smile. She continued walking with her head up and ignoring his ego.

"Hi. I would love a regular coffee please."

As she handed the money, she waited and brushed her hair while looking around the place. Once her head was turned all the way, she noticed Dylan and a friend of his talking trash to some dude who was sitting at the table beside them. They laughed and kept whispering things to each other. She just glared at them. With enough sighting, she walked over and placed her hands on her hips.

"Ahh the famous talk behind back whispers. They never stay in the shadows for long, do they?"

"Man, this little princess is Samantha Shaw. I think you've heard plenty of things that I would know about her."

"Ugh, you're so pathetic."

"Yet the question remains. Why is there a pathetic piece of trash standing near me?"

"Mm, funny. Just know that picking on others who are only regular humans such as you and me, is never going to make you a better person."

"How about you do you and I'll do me." Samantha felt rage shoot up from her spine. Yet she managed to hold it back. But she knew where she was heading towards next. She reached in her purse and pulled out a journal. It was covered in blue, designer patterns, and solid leather material. It was titled *'Dylan's Journal.'*

"You know, I've never heard of Navarro. Was it just something that seemed to be a great palace for a....god?" Dylan's face grew in shock. Almost like the words couldn't even come out.

"Where did you get that? You have no right to read that, it's mine!"

Perfection Is Key

"Then why's it all about us? Constant talk about each of us as if we're a part of some spy mission." His friend stood up with a disgusted look.

"Wait, bro, you have a journal full of other people? Why?"

"I do not! It was at the time when I was 7."

"That's not what the last printed date says," said Sam with a smirk. Dylan grew in embarrassment and anger while his friend walked out in laughter. While Sam stood smiling at him, he grew close to her face.

"You think you're so clever huh? Like you've got all the pieces put together."

"Well, it's a fun game of chess. Your move."

"You have no idea what I'm capable of doing."

"Ahem. I think I do. And your game seemed to be played as if you needed the instructions. But it was fun while it lasted." He remained silent. "Now, I'd suggest you just leave town and never ever look back. Otherwise, I'll publish this thing to the whole school." She grabbed her coffee and headed out.

It became noon one day. Dylan sat on a bench with his music playing and he scrolled through his phone. Ryan just happened to be running blocks. He ended up catching sight of Dylan. He headed toward him and sat down next to him. It was awkward. The two were never buddies ever since the day Dylan went all wild on Zander. They would bump heads just for the slightest things. At the same time, Ryan had a heart. He had one for Dylan. Just not so much faith.

"So..." Dylan continued scrolling as the awkward stares rolled through.

"So.." he continued.

Christopher Martinez

"Aha...look man, I know things have been very crazy between us two, but from now on, I promise to be very stable with my fellow frenemies."

"Dude, it's alright. I get why you had issues with me. I mean, I need to better my words and actions and even thoughts. It just takes time. I promise I'm getting better."

"Come to Zander's party tonight. He's just celebrating his Senior Year. I'm sure you can make some more friends. Or even regain them back."

"Alright. I'll go, but I know I'll be the most hated guy in that house." Ryan laughed it off and patted his shoulder. He then stood up and placed his headphones back in. Dylan looked up at him.

"Thank you for the pep." Ryan smiled and ran off.

Liam always grew nervous around Dylan due to him being the king and the scariest in the land. He was just a pet in Dylan's eyes.
It was a beautiful sunny day. Liam was at home, finishing up some designs on his new clothes. His phone rang as he answered it to Dylan.

"Hello?"

"Ay man, what's up! How are you doing these days, it's been a long while since we've talked."

"Gee, I wonder why."

"Ah c'mon man, don't be such a pity. Listen, I need a favor."

"Depends."

"I need a new outfit. Just for a family occasion I'm having. I just need something nice and simple. Not too fancy."

"Sure. Just one catch, it's fifty bucks." Dylan grew in shock and froze for a bit with his mind processing what he just heard.

"I'm sorry. What do you mean, fifty bucks?"

"It means I'm charging you."

Perfection Is Key

"What? Quit playing man. Just have it ready by Tuesday, alright?"

"Okay. But I'm still charging you."

"Liam. What's gotten into you? You do designs for free!"

"For people who actually deserve rewards such as my designs."

"Bro, just give me the design, please. I'll never ask again."

"And you'll never have to if you don't pay."

"Bro, c'mon."

"Sorry."

"You're being a jerk right now man."

"Well, I did learn from the best." Liam hung up with fury and felt no shame whatsoever. After all, Dylan was a complete jerk to him. All those years of torture and pain was just making Liam fed up. He had enough.

When it came to Tuesday, Dylan knocked upon Liam's door and had the money ready in his hands. The door swung open as Liam stood happily to see Dylan follow orders.

"Here. Now can I have my clothes?"

"You know, I'm surprised you actually brought the money. Knowing you, you'd fight me just to get your hands on the outfit."

"Yeah? I wished I could." Liam chuckled as he handed the design in a bag over. "Perfect man! Thank you. I owe you."

"Duh."

"But why did I have to pay? I mean, I understand why, but...why?"

"Look, there's the stories and there's the rumors. The world can rewrite it and change it and even read it, and it will probably inspire people to do good."

"So, what are you saying?"

Christopher Martinez

"That maybe the world would be better without those stories. More specifically, without you." He slammed the door as Dylan felt his pride get so wounded and his heart fall as if someone had just shot him. But Liam wasn't being a jerk. He meant that he would feel better if Dylan changed and became a better person. The pain filled his heart. He slowly walked away and headed home.

Everyone has a story. Everyone has something they want to share and help change the world, and there are those who want to stay behind a shadow and fall alone.

As we live on this earth, doing wrong or focusing too much on work or other business, we must remember to check up on our fellow people. Family, friends, strangers, addicts, etc. The world is full of creatures who seem to have a pretty face and look, but behind it all, they have a plate that's filled with broken hearts and shattered dreams. We want change? We must be the change and make this planet better. We must start by being a leader for those who can't lead at a certain moment.

People make mistakes. Usually, they learn from those who did wrong towards that person. They intend to think that's what life's about, but it isn't. If we stick together and play as a team, the winners make the greatest treasures from not only metal, but gold. Make every moment count.

Dylan Anderson. Gone, but never forgotten.

Chapter Twenty
Future Gifts

Life can change up anything in just any moment. It seems like once you look around, things seem to be normal. When in all reality, we must rub our eyes and see that everything has changed. Within a quick snap, people can be gone, and we think of it as nothing, but a part of life. Dylan was in great description when it came to who and how he was towards everyone. You never necessarily needed to know him or even meet him. By a great story, it's like you already knew who he was your entire life.

The gang hung out at a pizza place, talking amongst each other about their crazy journeys they experienced with Dylan personally.

"I'm still a little freaked out about Dylan's death. It's scary to hear that someone commits suicide before your graduation day," said Samantha.

"I know. I honestly hate to say it, but I feel like I can still feel him. Like if his soul still lingers around us. No matter where I go, his presence is there." said James.

"Dylan was just one of the guys. Now he's up in heaven. All we can do is hope that he's finally at peace," said Zander.

"Look let's just focus on something different. I know that we've just been through sort of a rough patch, but that doesn't mean we have to drown ourselves. Like, what about our careers? What do you guys plan to do now? I know I'm headed towards getting my own place

Christopher Martinez

and possibly opening up my own clothing store." Liam said with a smile.

They continued talking the rest of the afternoon. Friends can make a great outcome when they stay true to others and especially to themselves. Life can be way better when you have a great, beautiful, elegant circle of friends.

It was Dylan's funeral day. The coffin laid front and center as everyone sobbed. Most of the students who knew Dylan stood with a serious expression. The gang didn't want to deal with some drama, so they walked away eagerly.

Then came the time to pour the dust upon the coffin. Each one poured some with sobbing tears. While pouring the dirt, everyone stared at them in disgust and anger as they also gossiped.

Let's move on now, shall we? It was a fresh new week for each person. Samantha was just at home, helping her mother with the dishes and cleaning up the rest of the house. While helping her prepare dinner, she felt her stomach feel a little heavy.

"Sweetie, are you okay? You've seemed a bit off lately. Are you getting cramps again or anything? I know it seems like the end of the world, but you can do this. I'm here for all the support. I promise."

"Aha, thanks mom, but I'm fine. I've just been feeling very ill lately. I promise it's nothing serious though, so don't worry." As Sam took a small break, her mother continued cleaning on her own for a bit while keeping an eye out. Samantha felt dizzy and a bit sick. She would drink water and it would help a little bit, but otherwise, she felt as if she needed to throw up like every five minutes.

Perfection Is Key

At a random moment, she suddenly tipped over and fell off the couch. Her mother rushed on over in worry.

"Sweetheart what's going on? Are you okay? Talk to me. What's going on?!"

"I think my water broke."

She was rushed to the hospital as they put her in a room and checked up on her. There were tubes everywhere. Connecting either from machines or her body. Samantha's breathing became a little heavy. Contractions started and she felt as if lightning was striking her over and over. Her mother was texting and calling everyone she knew for all the support. Zander was the only one in a panic.

"How is she doing? Is everything okay?" Zander asked in a worried tone. He burst through the door as Samantha's mother held onto him.

"Yes, yes, my dear. She's just getting ready for birth. I told them to allow you in there when they're ready so that she isn't alone. I figured she would want you in there too."

"Ohh man, it's crazy that this is happening already," he said.

Zander had a nice childhood. It was never too easy though. He still had school and other friends to talk to and other events to attend. He was beginning to feel nervous about seeing the baby being born in an early time of his life. No one is ever ready to be a parent at a very young age, but when evil gets in the way of your plans, you do what you have to do.

Zander felt excited, yet he felt super nervous, but he knew he could do his best for his child. He had his girlfriend, his family, and even his best friends.

After a while, everyone was allowed in the room. They stepped in and their smiles were glistening in the sunlight. Zander held onto Samantha as she was holding her child. A healthy, beautiful baby girl. It was a sight of a beautiful family.

Christopher Martinez

"Everyone I would like you to say hi to our newest member, Ezra Robbins," said Sam. They all smiled as they watched her peacefully sleep in her mother's arms.

James on the other hand had thought of the idea of rekindling his relationship with Olivia's mother. It was a month after Ezra was born, and James had the courage to stand on Olivia's porch and ring her doorbell. The anxiety sent chills down his spine. He breathed deeply and stared at the door. It opened as Olivia's face grew in shock. She shut the door at a crack.

"What on earth are you doing here? You know that once my mother sees your face, she will freak out and beat you to death! You shouldn't be here."

"Look, that's why I came here, I want to talk to her and work things out. I want to show her something. Something that'll blow her mind and make her understand that I, James Coleman, am NOT a rebel. Plus, Zander is waiting in the car if she wants someone to prove how I've become a better man." Liv stared deep into his eyes as she then felt her heart jump up and down like crazy. Like if she had never seen such a nice man. Her mother hollered from afar.

"Liv who is it? Do you need me to come help?"

"No no, it-it's okay. Just making some small talk!" She decided to invite him in while keeping him quiet. She walked over to the kitchen where her mother was chopping some lettuce. She turned her attention toward Liv.

"Hey, who was at the door?" she asked.

"Mom, I know this is going to sound crazy for you to understand and you'll probably hate it, and...who knows what, but I have a guest who would like to speak to you. He just wants you to listen and understand him. Please, don't fail me now. Not when I finally get this close."

"Aha, sweetie, you know that whoever you bring into this home, I will be okay with. I promise not to freak out." She smiled as she grew nervous with her mother's words. Even though she was a grown, young, beautiful woman, she was afraid of her own mother at most times. Things would get hectic when it came to her holding anger towards someone or something.

As she then breathed heavily, she gestured to James to come on over. He revealed himself and he smiled with his head bowed a bit. Mrs. Lovington smiled back faintly as she then placed her hands on her hips.

"James."

"Mrs. Lovington. It's nice to see you. You're looking swell."

"Don't do that. Kissing my butt isn't going to make the sun burn any brighter."

"Mom," said Olivia.

"I'm sorry. I'm sorry, I just have a lot going through my head right now."

"Mrs. Lovington, I understand that you can't even stand my presence here in your house, but I swear I can show you that I've changed, and if you don't want to believe it, just watch this."

"Just as long as you know that I might not like you completely no matter what kind of kindness you do. When I know someone, I know them."

Her glare was like staring at a witch with glowing eyes and she could strike you down with one little spell. James got down on one knee and pulled out a ring. Olivia covered her mouth as her mother's eyes widened. He looked her deep in her eyes, smiled greatly at her, and spoke. The ring was not just any ring, it was a ring that

Christopher Martinez

represented both engagement and promise. The two were going to get married and he was promising her his entire life until death.

"Olivia Lovington, this ring was not just earned, or just bought, or even just honored, it was given and blessed for me to provide for you, my love. The day we met, it was crazy that I would find a woman such as you who would do anything for me, and I will love you more than yesterday and love you more tomorrow."

Her mother was in such a state of shock, it was too crazy to believe, but she knew what she was headed for. She knew what James was trying to imply with his words of wisdom and love. He did his best to prove his love for her and he wanted a great impression from her mother. People make mistakes. The true key is to learn from them. James continued.

"So even though I have no rich life, no great load of fancy cars, no fancy lifestyle in any sort of way you wish for or even desire, I can guarantee that I will lay down my life for you and make it the best one for the both of us and have a great life! It will take a while to get it all in good shape, but I swear it will be worth it for the rest of our lives. We have a whole future ahead of us and we deserve more than what we have now!"

"Oh my goodness, James...this is new! I don't even know what to say!"

"Just say yes," said Mrs. Lovington. Olivia looked at her mother with a great smile as she then took the ring and placed it on her finger.

Things can change in a split second, so we must take all the precious moments that we have now and make it the best we have! There's nothing wrong with being confident and taking risks. Life has more to it and it's better when you water it and improve it.

Perfection Is Key

After about a year, the two love birds ended up marrying and moving to Colorado with the blessing of Olivia's mother and his parents. Life was all in great shape for the two. James never thought of himself as a true lover until today. He'd learned a lot in the past.

He had changed from being crazy obsessed with making everyone stay fit and firm to being a kind young man at the heart of gold.

Olivia managed to begin her career as a nurse while James started his own business and opened a fitness center.

As for Liam, he ended up finishing college and opened his own clothing store and pursued his career in fashion. He was the young man who looked at clothes as too basic on a person even if they wore the most elegant clothing. Everyone would stiffen just by the passing of him. Everyone always did their best to impress him as they walked by him.

But now that he left the P3 group, he learned a lot as well, and realized how cruel his ego was. He knew now that there was no reason to judge another by what they're wearing and that it's all about the inside. He also learned that it's okay for everyone to walk a whole day feeling the best way.

Otherwise, people would dress as a regular teen person. The world is already ugly, so why should pretty have to be perfect?

Liam remained single most of the time. He never really paid attention to wanting a relationship. He wanted to focus more on his career and his clothing store. But things had other plans for him. He had a young woman walk into his store and look around for a beautiful dress.

Every time she stared at a dress, she'd lay it on her body and stare at herself with disgust in the mirror. Liam stared at her for a while. He finally walked up to her.

Christopher Martinez

"Hey there! How are you doing?" he asked.

"Uhm, I'm fine, I'm just looking around," she said nervously.

"Well, I'm sure you´ll find something. This store's open to everyone. You can pick anything you want. I can bet that you'll look amazing in it." She smiled faintly.

With Liam throwing these positive vibes around her, she was beginning to blush. But what he didn't realize was that she was a student at Rampage High who also feared him and hated him.

"Why are you being so nice to me?" she asked.

"Come again?"

"Do you not remember me? I was the girl you taunted for months in chemistry class. You always said I was legit a nobody with the way I dressed. You told me that what I wore was just suggested out of the dumpster and that it's so cheap like my life."

Liam stood in shock. All the memories came flooding back to his mind. He laughed a bit and slowly held her hand. She shivered a bit and took a small step back as she just stared back at him.

"No, it's okay. I was a mean jerk to you back in school. I was vain myself. I relied on looks. But I promise you, I've changed, things have been hectic, and I'm no longer a slave to P3 or even Dylan." She stared at him and worried for her life.

"Look, let me tell you something. I don't want you to ever think you can never shop here. I, Liam Dixon, have changed completely. Believe it or not, but I have. So has James. P3 doesn't exist anymore, and Dylan is gone. It may take time for many others to believe, but I'm willing to wait. I want my friends to come here and love their size and color and gender or whatever!! Their happiness is my key that I want to gain. So please, make it worth your time! Everyone who steps through my doors is always looking fabulous! So, understand this and appreciate it, you are enough."

Perfection Is Key

Charlotte smiled as she then gave him a giant hug. As he smiled and held her back, she was enlightened to feel like she had become free from a certain chain that was holding her back. She let go and stared into his eyes again, she stuttered and spoke.

"Um, I know this is going to sound...crazy, but do you have a girlfriend, or are you seeing anyone?"

"Hm depends, are you available for coffee tonight?" She chuckled at him as he smiled back.

"Yes."

"Then yes, I am seeing someone." They gave each other cute smiles as she then brushed her hair back.

"Well I'll see you tonight I guess?"

"Definitely."

She stepped out and headed back home, Liam stood aside and realized that he had gained a crush. I mean, she was pretty. She had long brown hair, hazel brown eyes, and a smile that could light up anyone's world. She always had the style of wearing the cutest clothes in the streets. She would wear leather jackets layered with white buttons along the edges. Something designed or plain under it with black skinny jeans with a few tears around it.

We come back to Ryan Williams. The best friend and best supporter anyone could ever have. He ended up finishing college while also meeting a girl and dating her and up to now, has had two kids with her. Cassie Williams and Dawn Williams.

"Girls let's go!! It's only been a month of school and you guys are already running late in the mornings. Let's move it along now!"

"Oh sweetie, remember to give them their lunches. I'M HEADED OUT NOW GIRLS! HAVE A GOOD DAY AT SCHOOL," said Mrs.

Christopher Martinez

Williams. Cassie came down the stairs as she was stuffing papers into her backpack.

"Sorry Dad! I was just getting all my folders and papers together. Mrs. Florez wants us to write like ten papers and it's a bit stressful to put them altogether. Might as well assign us the entire textbook." The family was in great shape and lived normal, stressful, crazy, positive lives. The Williams household was filled with Faith, Hope, and even Love. What more could they want?

As of last, but certainly never least, Zander Robbins. Zander ended college and grew his life with Samantha as they worked hard to support their child and each other. He became a mechanic. One position in life he never thought he would have seen himself in.

Overall, though, it was worth it. He wanted to do whatever it would take to support his family. It was better than nothing.

One day, Zander came home, and he walked up to his wife and daughter who sat in the kitchen, waiting for him to start dinner. They were both happy to see him. He sat down in front of his daughter and put down a toy house on the counter. Ezra was a bit confused by what she was seeing.

"What did you build daddy?" she asked.

"Ezra, I want to tell you something. Something so special that I hope it stays in your heart forever. Can you promise me that?"

"Yes." The house had a dark cloud over it, with thunder sounds, lightning flashes, and rain drops moving up and down.

"Look at the house. You see how it's covered in different pretty colors?"

"Yeah…"

"And you see how there's flowers and little statues of princesses and a bright light inside?"

Perfection Is Key

"Yeah..."

"Well, that's you. You're the pretty, gorgeous house that is filled with strength and light for the whole world to see." She smiled brightly at him. Samantha stared at her and then back at Zander.

"Now, there's going to be times when you come across bad days. The cloud is a land that may look like any cloud, but it could be carrying the ugliest things." He held her hand as she held him tightly and tried her best to understand what exactly he was trying to teach her. He continued. "You'll come across the rain. Where they will want to make you sweat out all your flaws and drain you from yourself. They want the world to see how you became the perfect queen. You'll then come across lightning. Where they will want to rip you from your 'trashy' clothing and turn you into something flashy. You'll lastly come across the thunder. Where the top ruler, who crowns themselves as queen and tries to make you selfish. All about you. It'll scream and roar until it is pleased with the pain and destruction it caused." Ezra lowered her head a bit in worry. He continued. "But don't worry though. You mind telling me what's missing from this whole thing?"

"Wind. Of course," she said with a smile.

"Right, the wind. Not only are you the pretty house, but you're also the wind. The three disasters that form this storm will tempt you into thinking you can join them and cause more destruction. Instead do the opposite and gently breathe yourself upon everyone and help them breathe your air calmly and gently. You understand me?"

"Yes. Don't worry daddy, I promise not to let anyone try to tear me down." Ezra was filled with courage and hugged her dad tightly as she took his project and kept it in a special place in her room. She looked at it every day to remind herself of what her father said.

"Wow. That sure is a way to teach a lesson about life. I didn't think you had it in you," said Sam as she patted his back and smiled in delight. It was a beautiful family. Life was amazing for the Robbins.

Christopher Martinez

"It looks so good by my bed," screamed Ezra as she jumped in place while clapping her hands. Her smile would warm her parents' hearts.

"Always walk like you're never alone," said Zander. They each hugged each other as Sam then passed out the dinner plates to prepare the food. They continued the night in joy as everything seemed...well, perfect.

Chapter Twenty-One
Take Notes

Zander Robbins was a great man. He had lived a crazy life, but in the end, he always found a way to make it look better and clean. He could bake you fresh cookies and tell the funniest stories. He made you feel welcome and safe. It would feel like you were in a home filled with wisdom and passion. He was the one man you could count on. The one man you could truly trust and honor.

So, the moral is...honor your life, and honor whoever laid down their life to take you in as their own. Don't ever think you are unworthy of everything and that you're something ugly or a piece of trash. You have more than your appearance. You're an art. And someday, not only will God place someone special in your life to appreciate you, but He'll also make sure you can learn and grow yourself. You're His art. That's something we should never forget.

You don't have to act like a jock or dress in the most modern clothing that makes you LOOK rich. You don't need to be fit to play sports or have working out as your only hobby. You don't have to be manly to keep your reputation. You are human too! You are enough.

Perfection will never be the key. Remember that and live those words. Teach the young what to expect and how they should respond kindly to it. You can make that change. It's not an easy route to take, but it's not an impossible one either.

In conclusion, I'm going to make my coffee and probably read some more books. This was such a great story to tell you fellow readers. Remember, always walk like you're never alone. Well, have a beautiful life.

Signed, Ezra Robbins.

Christopher Martinez

betterhelp.com

If you or a loved one struggle with mental illness, Better Help gives all the support and encouragement the best way possible! You are not alone; you are loved, and you are wanted. You're here right where you belong.

suicidepreventionlifeline.org

If you or a loved one are fighting suicidal thoughts, or battling depression, you can contact Suicide Prevention Lifeline for all the support and help! It is free and confidential! Remember you are needed in this world.

Christopher Martinez

I would love to acknowledge:

First and foremost, Thank You God! He blessed me enough to be able to share this story. He is always with us, and He is always so supportive, of course. I wouldn't have made it this far without Him. He sure dragged me out of this mental stage, and I couldn't be more grateful!

Thank you to my parents for all the support and for the advice on what I could do for such a future! You are both amazing and I hope to continue to make you proud! I love you both!

Thank you to my siblings for the encouragement and support as well. I wouldn't be doing what I do without you guys. We are always supporting each other's journeys, and their reactions to my stories continue to motivate me! Both the likes and dislikes! I love you all!

And last, but never the least, my awesome friends who have also supported the dream of this message and understood what message I wanted others to learn from it. There wasn't one moment where you stopped supporting or encouraging. And after all the times of pouring my dramas into your hands, you all kept up my hopes and my Faith! You kept reminding me of my potential. I love you guys!

Christopher Martinez

Christopher Martinez

is a self-published author coming from Muleshoe, Texas. He wrote his first book, *Perfection Is Key*, based off an inspirational poem he wrote back in 2019.

His stories are full of twists, drama, suspense, and mystery. But he writes for both a message to teach and entertainment.

Whenever Christopher isn't writing a new novel, he enjoys his time at work, spending time with his family, singing in his Church Choir, and reading.

You can follow his fan page on Facebook, and find him on Instagram, along with his other links, and even email him. Thanks for your awesome support!

Christopher Martinez